END RESULT

M. A. COMLEY

D1534031

OTHER BOOKS BY
NEW YORK TIMES BEST SELLING AUTHOR
M. A. COMLEY

Blind Justice (Novella)
Cruel Justice (Book #1)
Mortal Justice (Novella)
Impeding Justice (Book #2)
Final Justice (Book #3)
Foul Justice (Book #4)
Guaranteed Justice (Book #5)
Ultimate Justice (Book #6)
Virtual Justice (Book #7)
Hostile Justice (Book #8)
Tortured Justice (Book #9)
Rough Justice (Book #10)
Dubious Justice (Book #11)
Calculated Justice (Book #12)
Twisted Justice (Book #13)
Justice at Christmas (Short Story)
Prime Justice (Book #14)
Heroic Justice (Book #15)
Shameful Justice (Book #16)
Immoral Justice (Book #17)
Unfair Justice (a 10,000 word short story)
Irrational Justice (a 10,000 word short story)
Seeking Justice (a 15,000 word novella)
Clever Deception (co-written by Linda S Prather)
Tragic Deception (co-written by Linda S Prather)
Sinful Deception (co-written by Linda S Prather)
Forever Watching You (DI Miranda Carr thriller)
Wrong Place (DI Sally Parker thriller #1)
No Hiding Place (DI Sally Parker thriller #2)

Cold Case (DI Sally Parker thriller#3)
Deadly Encounter (DI Sally Parker thriller #4)
Lost Innocence (DI Sally Parker thriller #5)
Web of Deceit (DI Sally Parker Novella with Tara Lyons)
The Missing Children (DI Kayli Bright #1)
Killer On The Run (DI Kayli Bright #2)
Hidden Agenda (DI Kayli Bright #3)
Murderous Betrayal (Kayli Bright #4)
Dying Breath (Kayli Bright #5)
The Caller (co-written with Tara Lyons)
Evil In Disguise – a novel based on True events
Deadly Act (Hero series novella)
Torn Apart (Hero series #1)
End Result (Hero series #2)
In Plain Sight (Hero Series #3)
Double Jeopardy (Hero Series #4)
Sole Intention (Intention series #1)
Grave Intention (Intention series #2)
Devious Intention (Intention #3)
Merry Widow (A Lorne Simpkins short story)
It's A Dog's Life (A Lorne Simpkins short story)
A Time To Heal (A Sweet Romance)
A Time For Change (A Sweet Romance)
High Spirits
The Temptation series (Romantic Suspense/New Adult Novellas)
Past Temptation
Lost Temptation

KEEP IN TOUCH WITH THE AUTHOR:

Twitter
https://twitter.com/Melcom1

Blog
http://melcomley.blogspot.com

Facebook
http://smarturl.it/sps7jh

Newsletter
http://smarturl.it/8jtcvv

BookBub
www.bookbub.com/authors/m-a-comley

This book is dedicated to my rock, Jean, whose love and devotion is my guiding light.

Special thanks to my wonderful editor Stefanie. Thanks also to Joseph my superb proofreader.

And finally, my eternal thanks, go to Karri Klawiter for the wonderful cover as always, you're a very talented lady.

The images on the cover are provided by the super talented Craig Gillan.

PROLOGUE

Disorientated, Stuart Daws left the pub and stumbled towards the small terraced house he shared with his wife, Cathy. During the course of the evening, he'd consumed a couple of pints too many and was dreading Cathy getting home from work in a few hours. He didn't need a crystal ball to tell him the kind of reception he'd get when she saw the state of him. Cathy had no doubt already discovered the housekeeping pot empty. He cringed, imagining the screaming fit ahead of him. *But what the heck? I've a right to drown my sorrows now and again, don't I?* Never mind that it was mostly his missus's hard-earned money that filled the pot anyway.

The wind picked up, and ordinarily, it wouldn't have been fierce enough to affect him much. That night was different, though. He struggled to stand upright, and remaining on course also proved to be a daunting task—the bruises on his elbows were evidence of that. He cursed as he tripped over another crack in the pavement and added yet more bruises to his already painful arm. He nearly jumped out of his skin when an oncoming car blasted its horn, warning him to get out of its path.

He took the shortcut that ran between several terraces whose yards backed onto each other. He used it frequently to get home from the pub, but in the dark and with no nearby streetlights to guide him, he reached out to feel his way up the alley. Stuart foolishly overlooked the bin lying in his path and cried out when his shin smashed against the metal.

"Ssshhh, you mangy mutt. You'll wake the neighbourhood," he slurred at the dog growling at him from behind the six-foot brick wall to one of the gardens.

He continued to stagger onwards, guided by the dimmest of lights from one of the houses towards the end of the alley. Concentrating hard on keeping himself upright, he neglected to hear the person sneaking up behind him. Before Stuart had a chance to react, his assailant had wrapped something around his neck, cutting off his airway.

His ears filled with the sound of his own choking. He tried to slide his fingers under the cord eating into his flesh, but it tightened and sliced through the flesh of his fingers. Such excruciating pain. His hands were now caught, trapped under the wire, leaving him only his legs to defend himself with. He kicked out awkwardly at his attacker, but once one of his feet left the ground, he lost his balance and fell heavily against the wall.

"Get... off... me!" The words he'd intended to shout came out a long way short of a whisper.

With Stuart on his knees, the attacker's job became much easier, and his hold over the drunken man intensified. Stuart felt his attacker pull the wire tighter by crossing his hands at the back of Stuart's head, totally depriving him of oxygen. Stuart's body gave up the will to fight off his aggressor, and he went limp. Just before he lost consciousness, he heard the attacker run off. *Stay awake, Stu! Someone will find me soon enough if only I can stay awake.*

It proved to be an impossible task, and within seconds, Stuart's eyes fluttered shut for a final time. His life ended at the tender age of twenty-seven.

CHAPTER ONE

Hero ran through the incident room, issued orders to his team about what he expected them to do in his absence, then bolted down the stairs to the car park.

"Good luck, Hero." The desk sergeant's voice followed Hero out the front door as he bounded down the steps.

"I'm going to need it, but not as much as Fay," he mumbled as he pressed the button on his key fob to unlock the car. He had been expecting the call all morning, but nothing really prepared anyone for fatherhood. He toyed with the idea of placing the police light on the roof of his car and using his siren to make his trip to the hospital quicker. Then he decided he'd been in enough trouble over the years with his bosses, and he'd promised Fay he would mend his ways and settle down once the twins were born. Just as that time was arriving, he was already thinking of going against his word. He slid into the traffic at the junction and sat impatiently drumming his fingers while the vehicles moved as if they were part of a slow-motion movie.

"Get a bloody move on, guys! My wife's in labour, for God's sake."

When he finally arrived at the hospital, he gave a tenner to the parking attendant stationed in the little hut and asked him to keep an eye on his car. In the hospital, he followed the yellow line on the hallway floor that led to the maternity unit. Hero pushed open the door and rushed up to the young nurse on duty.

"My wife's in labour. Fay Nelson. Where do I go?"

She smiled. "If you'd like to come with me, sir."

Hero followed the nurse down another corridor to a private room. Just as the nurse opened the door, Fay screamed out in pain.

Nervously, Hero approached the side of the bed, shrugged awkwardly at the two nurses already in the room, and gripped Fay's hand. "I'm here, love."

Large beads of sweat glistened on his wife's forehead. Hero pulled out his linen handkerchief and wiped her brow.

"I'm glad you made it before the buggers come out," Fay joked as a contraction took hold.

"We can't christen both of them by that name. What do you want to call the other one?" His attempt to alleviate her pain with humour seemed to work for the briefest of moments before yet another contraction came.

"Okay, Mr. Nelson, we think the babies are about to make an entrance. Be prepared for your hand to have the life squeezed out of it," the midwife said light-heartedly.

Hero nodded at the midwife and held Fay's hand between both of his. "I love you, Fay, and our troublesome twosome."

"It's a good job I love you, Hero Nelson. Just to make things perfectly clear, this is never going to happen again."

He kissed her on the lips and swept the damp hair off her forehead. "Hey, whatever you want to do is fine by me. Is Louie with your mum?"

"Yes. I said you'd call as soon as... ugh!" Fay yelled before she started pushing.

"Okay, don't talk. I get the gist," he replied, wishing he could take on some of his wife's excruciating pain. He watched in awe as his beloved wife dealt with the birth, taking all the poundings the twins were intent on dishing out. He cringed and crossed his legs the whole way through and marvelled at the pain threshold women were forced to exceed during the ordeal of childbirth.

Fay heaved, and the first baby came into the world, crying. She glanced at him and smiled briefly before she pushed out the second twin.

"Have you decided on names yet?" the midwife asked as she handed him a clean baby girl wrapped in a blanket.

Hero gazed down at the fragile bundle, tears misting his eyes, rendered speechless by the lump the size of a huge boulder settling in his throat.

As the other nurse handed the second baby to her, Fay said, "Zoe and Zara."

"That's lovely. I hope the four of you will be healthy and happy together." The midwife rubbed Hero's arm and tucked the blanket away from the baby's face. "She won't break."

"I know. The thing is, I've never held a baby before," Hero confessed. "Fay has a son—I mean, we have a son at home already, but Fay had him with another man. What I should have said is..."

"Hero, shut up. You're rambling. Just enjoy the moment," Fay chided him good-naturedly.

The midwife left the room, laughing, while the other nurse cleared away the dirty towels.

Hero shrugged at his wife. "Sorry."

She leaned over to kiss him. "You're forgiven, under the circumstances. You better go and ring Mum and your mum and dad. The nurse will stay with me for a few more minutes, won't you?"

Hero glanced up at the nurse, who nodded, then turned back to Fay. "Will you be all right holding both of them?"

Fay nodded, and he handed her the daughter he was holding then kissed the three of them before leaving the room.

In his state of elation, he walked through the hospital, sucking in gulps of fresh air before he telephoned his parents.

"Mum, you have two new granddaughters."

"Oh, how wonderful. We'll be right over. Is everything okay with Fay?"

"Yeah, they're all fine and beautiful, Mum."

"I'm so proud of you, son. Give our love to Fay, and we'll see you soon."

Next on his list to ring were Fay's mum and Louie. "Deirdre, Zoe and Zara have made an appearance, at last."

His announcement was greeted by a whoop of joy. "Congratulations, the pair of you. How's Fay?"

"Exhausted, but elated. The girls are the spitting image of her."

"Louie was the same when he was born. Come here, darling, Daddy wants to speak to you."

Louie came on the line. "Hello, Daddy."

"Hello, son. I'm pleased to announce that you have two new playmates."

"Wow, how cool. Grandma and me made ice cream. We could bring some if you like. The babies might like it."

Hero chuckled. "I think it might be a bit cold for their bellies, son. Maybe in a few months, eh?"

"All right. If it lasts that long. When can I meet them?"

"Put Grandma back on the phone, and we'll make arrangements, okay?"

Deirdre asked, "When can we visit?"

"Anytime you want to. I'm going to be here the rest of the day— sod work for a change. Do you want me to send a taxi to fetch you?"

"That'd be great. Louie would love that. Ask the driver to pick us up in half an hour. It'll give me time to clean him up. He got carried away in the kitchen, and the ice cream went everywhere. He's rather grubby."

"That sounds like Louie, all right. I'll contact the taxi firm now. See you soon."

The final call Hero made was to his sister. "Cara, we're at the hospital. Fay's had the twins, both of them girls, as the scans predicted."

"Aww… that's great, Hero. How are they all?"

"Smashing. Come in later if you like. How's the training going?" Cara had joined the Met and had been on a training course in Manchester for the last month or so.

"It's all right. I'm eager to get out there. Getting a little bored with the paperwork side of things."

Hero snorted. "Hey, get used to it, love. There'll be a lot more of that when you join the force proper."

"Yeah, that's what the instructor told us. I'll come in after I've finished here. Around sixish, okay?"

"Look forward to it, Sis. Don't overwork those brain cells, will you?"

"Fat chance of that happening here," Cara grumbled.

Hero had warned his sister that the training would be an endless source of frustration. They had joined the Territorial Army together, and Hero knew her skills would be invaluable and easily adaptable to the Manchester Police Force—if she could manage to get past the training without a hitch.

"Come over on Saturday. There's no TA this weekend anyway, and we'll discuss your training then if you like?"

"Thanks for the offer, bruv, but I think you'll have your hands tied with the little ones. Ignore me. I'll get past this grumpy stage, I hope. You go, get back to your family. I'll see you later. Send my best wishes to Fay."

"If you're sure, hon? See you this evening."

Hero hung up and walked, or rather, *skipped* back to the maternity unit, unaware of the huge grin he was sporting. Life was good, the best it had been in years. Outside the room, he watched Fay lovingly gaze down at the two bundles in her arms. *Life doesn't get better than this.*

Cara was the last family member to visit. Fay looked shattered despite smiling through her exhaustion as each relative turned up at the hospital to see the new arrivals. The twins had been asleep in the cots beside the bed for hours.

At eight o'clock, Hero kissed his wife on the lips and told her good-bye. "I'll see you tomorrow, love. Get some sleep now. You look done in."

Fay gave him a weak smile and snuggled down in the bed. "I'll try. I hope you get some rest, too."

Cara accompanied Hero home that evening, and they were just about to tuck into the fish and chips they had picked up on the way back to the house when Hero's phone rang.

"Damn, it's work. I told them not to bother me unless it was important. I better answer this."

Cara waved her hand as she stuffed a few chips into her mouth. "Go ahead. Don't mind me."

"Hello?"

Julie Shaw, Hero's partner replied, "Sir, I thought I better ring you right away. We've got a dead body on our patch."

"Shit. And you're telling me you're not capable of handling this in my absence?"

"I just thought you should know, sir. I'm sorry to have disturbed you."

"It's all right, Julie. What's done is done. What have we got?"

"Found in an alley in Salford, the body of a man believed to be in his twenties."

"Anything else? Any witnesses? Is it a suspicious death? Give me a clue, Shaw, for goodness's sake?" Hero looked at Cara and rolled his eyes up to the ceiling. Covering the phone, he said to his sister, "See what I have to put up with?"

Cara sniggered and dipped a chip in her curry sauce.

Julie blew out an exasperated breath. "No witnesses. The man had consumed a large amount of alcohol shortly before his death."

"And you know that how?"

"By the fumes coming from his mouth, sir. Yes, it appears to be a suspicious death because the man was garrotted."

"Oh, I see. You better give me the address, and I'll take a wander out there. Are you packing up for the day?"

Shaw read out the address. "No. I'm heading over to the scene now. I'll meet you there if you like, sir."

Before he could respond, his partner hung up.

"I better finish this and get over there," he told his sister. Not that he had much appetite left after learning how the victim had perished.

"Is it a murder enquiry?" Cara asked, ripping off a piece of crispy-battered cod and putting it in her mouth.

"Looks that way. The victim was garrotted." After finishing his meal, Hero drove to the scene. He encountered an operation that was much larger than he'd expected. Holding up his warrant card, he dipped under the crime scene tape then went in search of his partner.

He located Julie leaning against a brick wall, wisely keeping out of the pathologist's way. Gerrard was known to be a bit of a grouch when he first arrived at a scene.

"Hi, do we know anything else yet?" Hero asked Julie as he came to a standstill beside her.

She pushed her elbow against the wall to stand upright. "Not yet. I'm waiting for the pathologist to give me the all-clear to proceed."

"Knowing Gerrard, we could be here quite a while then."

No sooner had he said the words than the pathologist whistled and motioned with his head for them to join him alongside the body. Forgetting the usual pleasantries of shaking hands, the three of them surveyed the body as Gerrard ran through the victim's injuries.

"My guesstimate at this early stage would be that the man was attacked from behind with some kind of wire. The marks—stroke *cuts*—to his fingers tell me that he tried to put up a struggle. More than likely, he raised his hands and hooked them under the wire to try to prevent it tightening around his throat. Being heavily intoxicated, I doubt he had the ability to put up much of a fight to defend himself."

"Do you think it was a mugging? Or was the attack something more sinister?" Hero asked, tilting his head from one side to the other as he studied the corpse.

"I'd say the latter. No sign of attempted mugging. I checked his pockets and found a few coins, and there was a ten-pound note in his wallet."

"Any ID?"

Gerrard shook his head. "Not that I could find."

"Great. Anything else of significance, Doc?"

"Not really. Of course, I'll know more once the examination has been carried out."

"Okay. Julie, can you take some pictures? Maybe the doc can turn the victim over for a second or two?"

"Sure, I've carried out all the necessary tests and evidence bagging I need to do." Gerrard gently eased the body over on the ground.

Julie inhaled a sharp breath.

"What's wrong? Do you recognise him?" Hero asked.

"No. I just don't like looking at someone once their throat is slit open like that."

Hero held out his hand. "Camera. I'll do it." He fired off several shots then handed the camera back to his partner. "Let's call it a day and start afresh tomorrow, all right?"

"I'll carry out the post mortem tomorrow and get back to you with the results, hopefully sometime in the afternoon, Inspector," Gerrard said before instructing his team to place the body in a bag.

Hero accompanied Julie back to where their cars were parked, bid her farewell, and drove home. Despite being on the wagon, he decided to pour himself a glass of brandy. He deserved a treat since he'd just become a proper father for the first time in his life.

CHAPTER TWO

The next morning, after calling in at the hospital for a brief visit with his family, who were all sleeping when he got there, Hero walked into the incident room to a round of applause from his colleagues. One of the older members of the team, Lance Powell, approached him, obviously as the spokesperson for the group. He awkwardly held out a cute four-inch teddy bear to Hero. "Umm… congratulations to you and Mrs. Nelson, sir. The team had a whip round and bought you this."

Hero stifled the smirk dying to escape and nodded as he accepted the toy. "Thanks, Lance. I'll make sure the twins don't fight over it."

Powell's face dropped, and he glanced over his shoulder at the team standing behind him. Several of the others raised a hand to cover their sniggers of embarrassment. Powell turned to face Hero again and shrugged. "Sorry, sir."

Hero patted Lance on the shoulder. "Never mind, Powell. It's the thought that counts. Thanks, everyone. Now let's get back to work. Julie, step into my office, will you?"

He heard Julie trotting behind him as he pushed open the door to his office and walked in.

After they were both seated, Julie took out her notebook, and Hero nodded for her to proceed.

"Well, I thought I'd run off the photos first thing and see if they match anyone on the database. I'll send uniformed officers around the area where the crime was committed today to start the house-to-house enquiries, just in case someone heard anything last night."

"Do we know the time of death?"

"The pathologist was uncertain about that, but he reckoned around seven or eight. Early enough for someone to have heard or witnessed something, I guess."

"If that's the case, it means the victim had probably spent the afternoon in a pub, a nearby pub, getting pissed. Either ring round or get someone to pay the pubs in the area a visit."

"Will do, sir." Julie rose from the table and left without saying anything further.

Before tackling his boring, mostly non-essential paperwork, Hero reflected on what they knew about the case so far. He started jotting down notes for possible motives for the attack, always the type to think of every probable angle during a case. Mugging had already been ruled out, unless the muggers had made off with a large sum of money and intentionally left the small stuff. That was a possibility. He also included "gang related" in his list. Hero had witnessed several heinous gang-turf crimes over the years. One of his most recent cases had been a prime example. He shuddered involuntarily at the thought of the notorious Krull Gang. In the end, they had attempted to bully the wrong person, and he'd made them pay as retribution for the loved ones the gang had murdered. Domestic dispute was always worth considering. Maybe his team should be considering some form of love triangle.

Mid-way through the morning, Hero finished his paperwork and went in search of his partner, to see what she'd managed to find out about the victim, if anything. Julie was the type who expected people to come to her for news about an investigation rather than volunteering the information as soon as she discovered anything relevant. It was a constant source of irritation to Hero, and he hadn't quite found a tactful means of correcting it. He perched on the desk next to Julie's. "What have we got?"

Without taking her eyes off the screen, she informed him, "I've got a name for the victim. At least, I think I have."

"And?" Hero asked with a tut, eager for her to tell him.

"Stuart Daws. He's on file as being a petty criminal."

"Okay, do you have an address for him?"

"Of course." Julie waved a piece of paper under his nose while still concentrating on the screen.

He resisted the temptation to snatch the rudely presented piece of paper from her. "Okay, let's get round to his place and see what we can find out. I take it he lived close to the scene of the crime?"

"Yep, a few streets away." Julie removed her jacket from the back of her chair and slipped it on.

"Anyone got anything else before we go?" Hero asked the rest of the team.

Sally, whom the team had nicknamed "Foxy" when she joined them a few years ago, glanced up and shook her head. "Not yet, sir. I sent PCs out to conduct house-to-house. I'm waiting for them to report back."

"Okay, Foxy. Leave it until lunchtime and chase them up, will you? There might be a witness out there, and that person just doesn't realise it."

"Yes, sir."

When Hero surveyed the rest of the room, other team members all had their heads down, focusing on their work.

"Jason, can you do an early sandwich run? I'm starving. We have to nip out now, but I'd like a sandwich waiting for me when we return. "I'll have a cheese and ham on white." Hero walked over and gave the youngest member of the team a twenty-pound note. Julie, what do you want?" he called over to his sour-faced partner.

"Tuna and mayo, thanks." She added the last word as an afterthought.

"See what everyone else wants, and be as quick as you can. Keep up the good work, folks."

"Yes, sir." Jason stood up and worked his way around the room with a pen and notepad in hand, taking the orders.

"Come on, Julie."

Hero and Julie left the station and drove to the victim's address.

"Something up?" Hero asked a few minutes into the journey.

"Nope."

Hero hated being lied to, and something was obviously wrong with Julie. He pressed her further, "Julie, I can tell when something's bugging you. Spill?"

Ignoring him, she stared at the white van in front of them.

Hero let her remain quiet for a second or two then insisted, "Come on. No bullshit this time. What's up?"

Julie rested her head against the headrest and exhaled a long breath. "It's Mum. The doctor told her that the cancer has spread. It's terminal."

"Shit. I'm sorry to hear that, Julie. There's nothing more the hospital can do? She's had chemo, *et cetera?*"

"Yep, they've tried everything."

Hero glanced sideways and saw Julie wipe away a large tear that had splodged onto her colourless cheek.

"Look, if you need to take time off to be with her, I can arrange it with the super." Guilt flushed through him for breezing happily into work after the birth of his twins, until he reprimanded himself for being daft. That was what life was all about, wasn't it? New lives began as others petered out and ended. In his partner's case, Julie's mother was barely sixty, far too young to say farewell to the world.

"I'd rather work. Mum's being cared for by the Macmillan nurse they've appointed her. I might have to take time off further down the road though, once her health starts to deteriorate."

"Just ask. I hope Rob is showing his support?"

Julie sighed and closed her eyes. Hero turned to see that she was chewing on her bottom lip. When she finally spoke again, her voice sounded strangled. "He's walked out on me."

Hero clobbered the steering wheel with his clenched fist. "I'm sorry about that, Julie. You know my thoughts on the man, a total waste of space in my book. The heartless piece of shit."

"The last thing I want to hear right now, sir, is 'I told you so.'"

"Okay, I know how you like to keep your personal life private. I'll just say one thing—there's no need to bottle things up, all right? My door is always open should you need a shoulder to cry on or time off to cope with the emotional baggage heading your way."

"Yes, sir. Thank you." Julie coughed and straightened her shoulders. "I think it's this road on the right." She pointed to a small turning up ahead of them.

Hero took the hint not to revisit the conversation. He doubted very much that Julie would take him up on his offer, but at least his conscience was clear. He'd offered her support in her time of need, unlike her bastard of a boyfriend. He shook his head and made a vow to have a word in the despicable constable's ear when time permitted. He'd never liked the little shit, and taking him down a peg or two would be a pleasure.

"Shake a leg, girl." Hero smiled, and they both got out of the car.

Julie appeared to be focused on the job in hand as she rang the doorbell of the grubby-looking terraced property.

Hero flashed his warrant card at the woman who opened the door. "Mrs. Daws? I'm DI Nelson, and this is DS Shaw. May we come in for a second?"

Dazed, the young woman, whose greasy brown shoulder-length hair looked as though it hadn't been combed—let alone washed—in days, stepped back behind the door and allowed them to enter. She led them through the house to a littered lounge that Hero suspected hadn't had an in-depth clean by either a duster or hoover in weeks. His keen nose twitched at the stale smell of alcohol invading his nostrils from the numerous beer cans littering the floor and table. *What a bloody tip! I've seen pig sties cleaner than this.*

"Is this about Stuart? I've been out of my mind with worry. He didn't come home last night." The woman hurriedly cleared a space for them on the sofa before plonking down on the beanbag opposite.

Hero nodded. "It is. I'm sorry, but I have some bad news."

"Is he in the hospital?" she asked, her eyes bulging with fear.

"In a manner of speaking, yes. I'm afraid your husband was found lying in an alley last night. He was dead."

She buried her face in her hands and howled. She rocked back and forth as the howl ebbed and flowed. It was a while before Mrs. Daws recovered enough to speak.

Hero watched the scene with a lump in his throat. He couldn't imagine what the woman must be feeling. He'd never lost anyone close before, and he could only imagine the pain she was going through.

"I'm sorry. Can I call someone to come and be with you?"

"No. There is no one. Only Stu… now he's gone and…" She looked up, tears glistening in her eyes. "What am I going to do? How will I survive without him, his money? They'll take all the benefits off me now. I'll have to move, to leave my home. This is the first place we've really felt settled."

"I'm sure the authorities will regard your case with sympathy."

"You're kidding me?" she said with a snarl. "The council round here is crying out for suitable homes to house yet more bloody immigrants. Now that Stu's gone, I'll be turfed out onto the streets." She started sobbing again.

Hero and Julie looked at each other in despair. *Really? That's this woman's first thought about her husband's demise? What's going to happen to her once word gets out about his death?* He cleared his throat. "Going back to your husband's death. Where was he last night?"

She narrowed her eyes. "If you're asking if he was on the rob, no. He ain't done nothing like that for months... hang on a sec'." She leapt out of her chair and left the room. She returned a few seconds later, holding a tin that appeared to be some kind of tea caddy. "I take that back. The bastard robbed me housekeeping money. The little shit!"

"Did he make a habit of dipping into that tin?" Hero asked, not bothered if the man had or not. It was irrelevant to his case, or was it? If Daws still had a considerable amount of money on him after leaving the pub, that would have been all the motive the killer needed.

"Now and again." She sank back into her beanbag and proceeded to light up a dog-end she'd fished out of an overflowing ashtray.

Hero shuddered at the thought of smoking something so close to the filtered tip. "So, I take it you have no idea if he was meeting anyone last night?"

"Nope. I was at work. When I got home, I expected him to be here, but he wasn't."

"And where do you work, Mrs. Daws?"

She looked at him and frowned. "What the fuck has that got to do with anything?"

"It's a simple question, Mrs. Daws. Do you earn money illegally? Is that why you're avoiding the question?"

"Of course I don't. You can't come in here like this and make disgusting insinuations like that." She threw her arms out to the side. "All right, I work as a barmaid."

Julie took out her notebook and started scribbling down the woman's details.

"Where?" Hero asked evenly, despite his growing frustrations.

"At the Dog and Duck in Moss Side."

Nice area... not. It doesn't really come as a surprise, looking at her.

"I see. Thank you. So, when was the last time you saw your husband alive, Mrs. Daws?"

She took a puff on the filter in her hand and vigorously stubbed the remainder out in the ashtray. "Yesterday, around lunchtime, I suppose."

"About one o'clock? Or later than that?"

She thought about her answer for a second or two. "About twoish then, if you're going to push me."

"Okay, well, your husband was found in an alley in the Longford Park area last night. Any idea what he was doing there?"

"Nope. In an alley, you say? Maybe he was practising his Peeping Tom act." She laughed at her own joke, however she quickly straightened her face and cast her eyes down to the floor when neither of the detectives joined in.

"Is there a regular pub he frequents in the area maybe?"

She clicked her fingers. "Yep, he likes to go down the New Inn. I reckon he fancies the busty blonde behind the bar. Anyways, I've told him to steer clear of my pub. I mean the pub where I work. He got me in bother with the boss when I snuck him a freebie beer once. I nearly got the sack because of it."

"I see. Was he in full-time employment?"

She snorted. "You're kidding? He don't know what work is, that one. Lazy git at the best of times. I'm the only breadwinner in this household."

"Okay, I thought you said you were on benefits before?"

An embarrassed glow settled into the woman's chubby cheeks. "Yeah, well, me and the benefits help run this gaff. That's what I meant."

"I'm glad we clarified that," Hero said smugly.

"Did your husband have any friends? Maybe he met up with them at the pub yesterday?"

"Naw, all his mates are like leaches down at the pub. If he's got money to burn, they swarm to him like flies around dog shit. If he was drinking with *my* housekeeping money, he would have been someone's best friend for the day down there. That's for sure."

"We'll call at the pub and find out. Does your husband have any enemies? Can you think of a reason why anyone would want to kill him?"

"I've threatened to a number of times, usually when he's robbed my money. Apart from drinking with the regulars down at the pub, he's a bit of a loner. He's never mentioned anyone being out to get him or anything like that, not as far as I can remember, anyway."

Hero dug a business card out of his jacket pocket and handed it to Mrs. Daws as he stood up. She struggled out of the beanbag and showed both the detectives to the front door.

"If you can think of anything that'll help our enquiries, please get in touch. We'll keep you up to date with our findings. Again, I'm sorry for your loss."

The second they stepped over the threshold, the front door slammed behind them.

"Charming," Julie grumbled as they made their way back to the car.

"Well? What did you make of that?" Hero knew what he'd made of the woman's performance, but he wanted to see if his partner felt the same. He was keen to make sure she was concentrating fully on the job, and he also wanted to find out if he was misjudging the grieving woman.

Once they were in the car, Julie found her voice. "She's weird. One minute, she was sobbing her heart out at her loss, and the next, she was more concerned about losing her home and the benefits she's on."

"Yeah, that didn't ring true with me, either. My take on it is that they didn't have a happy marriage. The lack of family photos was all the evidence I needed to come to that conclusion—there were none that I could see anyway. All that howling when I initially broke the news to her appeared to be for our benefit, agreed?"

"Definitely. Where to next? The New Inn, to see if he was drinking there last night?"

"That's my thinking. Maybe the regulars will open up to us and can shed some light on any enemies the victim might have had." Hero pulled out into the traffic and drove towards the pub. "Ring Foxy, will you? Ask her to track down the CCTV footage from last night in the alley area? Maybe we'll spot something on that."

"Okay." Julie rang the station and requested that Foxy carry out the task right away.

The pub car park was nearly empty when they arrived. "Let's hope that's the owner's car, or that it at least belongs to someone who worked the night Daws was here." Hero nodded towards a car, the only one sitting on the tarmac, parked close to the back door of the establishment.

They walked around the front of the pub and knocked on the door, and a tall bearded man with a very round beer belly opened it. "Yeah, what do you want? We're closed for another hour or so."

"I appreciate that. I'm DI Nelson, and this is DS Shaw. We'd like to ask you a few questions about an incident which happened in the vicinity last night, if that's all right?"

He studied Hero's warrant card carefully and thrust open the door so they could enter. He strode over to the large bar and hopped up onto one of the barstools. "All right, what incident are you talking about?"

"We believe one of your regulars was murdered last night."

The man's brow furrowed. "Yeah? Which one?"

"A Stuart Daws. Do you know him?"

"Yeah. Man, that's rough. He seemed in good spirits when he left here last night. Mind you, he was pissed."

Out of the corner of his eye, Hero saw Julie taking notes. "What time did he leave here? Can you tell us that?"

"Not sure of the exact time. The place was fairly busy last night, it was skittles night. I always put a mini-buffet on, so I was mostly out back in the kitchen."

"A guess will do then, if you don't mind. Just so we have a rough idea of when the crime took place."

"Around seven to seven thirty. How about that?"

"Do you know if there was any kind of trouble in here last night, involving Daws, I mean?"

"Not that I know of. He was buying several of the other regulars drinks. He kept teasing them but didn't mention where he'd got his windfall from."

"We know where the money came from. Perhaps you can give me a list of the names of his drinking partners?"

"Sure, I only know them by their first names. I have no idea where they live or anything like that to help you out."

"That's okay. Maybe I can get one of my team to come in later and question the regulars, just in case?"

The landlord's mouth twisted. "If you must. Can you make sure they do it discreetly? You know how it is when folks think the filth… sorry, the police are around? Word will soon spread, and trade will likely drop off."

"I can assure you my team will be discreet. The names?"

"Let me see… ah, yes, there's Stan. He was here all afternoon and joined Stuart about fourish. Then there's Mick. He's the only one of the three who has a job, so he turned up around five thirty. If you wanna question him, there's no point turning up before then."

"I'll make a note of that, thanks," Julie said.

Hero handed the man a card. "If you think of anything else, get in touch, yeah?"

The man took the card and placed it in front of a bottle of gin on the bar behind him. "Will do."

CHAPTER THREE

Back at the station, Hero checked up on the team's progress and actioned the afternoon's enquiries. "Lance, I need you to drop in and question a couple of the punters at the New Inn later." The man started to stand up, but Hero placed a hand on his shoulder, pushing him back down into his chair. "Later, as in on your way home. I think the pub is near your house, isn't it?"

"Ah, okay, yeah, that's right, sir. Any specific reason?"

Hero exhaled, showing his annoyance. Lance Powell wasn't the brightest member of his team. He was the type of officer who needed everything laid out in front of him before he started making any connections in a case.

"The New Inn was the last place our victim was seen alive, Lance. The landlord saw him drinking with two men. The thing is, we haven't got the surnames of these two men, so our hands are tied with regard to doing any background checks on them until that has been verified. That's where you come in. First, get their names and addresses then ask them what they know about Daws, not necessarily about his death, just general knowledge. You know, ask if he's had any bother lately with anyone, that sort of thing. His wife didn't think he had, but he might've let it slip to one of his mates. Until we get that information, our case is going to be hard to crack. His wife couldn't tell us much."

"I see. Okay, boss. I'll see what I can find out and report in tomorrow."

Hero sat on the edge of Foxy's desk. "Anything show up in the CCTV footage yet?"

"I've only just obtained the discs, sir. Hopefully, I'll get back to you soon."

"No problem. I'm eager to get going on this, so as quick as you can, all right?"

"Got it." Foxy inserted a disc into her computer and tapped a few keys.

"Was there any news on the house-to-house enquiries, Foxy?" He asked, making his way over to Jason.

"Nothing, sir. I find that hard to believe, considering the time of the attack, don't you?" Foxy called after him.

"Yes, it does seem very odd. Although given the neighbourhood, maybe the residents have become immune to the disturbances they hear early on in the evening. Maybe it would have been a different story if the incident had occurred early in the morning? Who knows with these things. It's frustrating, all the same."

Jason beat out a rhythm on the desk with his pen and reclined in his chair as Hero approached.

"Give Foxy a hand with the CCTV footage, will you?"

"Sure. Hopefully, we'll find what we're looking for if two of us are on it."

Hero agreed, walked in his office, and slumped into his chair. He picked up the phone and rang his mother-in-law to check how Louie was. "All right, Deirdre? Did Louie get off to school okay?"

"Hello, Hero. Yes, eventually. He's so excited, bless him. Lord knows how he managed to get any sleep last night."

Hero chuckled. "Yep, I know that feeling. I don't suppose you've rung the hospital today to see how Fay and the girls are doing, have you? I called in on my way to work this morning, but they were all sound asleep."

"Poor thing is bound to still be exhausted. I'll leave it until later on this afternoon then. The nurses will be constantly checking on her throughout the day, I should imagine. So if she's sleeping, I'll leave her be."

"That's what I thought. I'm going to call at the hospital on my way home this evening. Can't wait to see and hold them all."

"I'll let you go and do some work. Talk soon, Hero." Deirdre ended the call.

"Boss!" Foxy poked her head around the doorframe.

Hero jumped to his feet, knowing the sergeant wouldn't have interrupted him if she didn't have something urgent. "What have you got?"

"Something you should see on the CCTV footage," Foxy said as he followed her back into the incident room.

He leaned on the desk between Jason and Foxy and stared closely at the screen. "That's Daws, I take it?" Hero asked.

"Yep, the speculation about him being drunk was a little off the mark. I'd say he was totally inebriated. I'm surprised he knew which direction to take once he left the pub." Foxy tutted and began fast-forwarding through the images.

"Maybe he has some kind of in-built homing device, like most drunks seem to have," Jason offered.

"Okay, on this frame, he's staggering along the main road. I watched him take the side road and disappear. I thought that was it. However, I left the disc running, and *this* is what I found." Foxy pointed at a hooded figure who appeared to be following Daws into the side road.

"Interesting. Can you take the disc back?" Hero asked.

"I was just about to. The thing is, I was concentrating so much on Daws that I neglected to see this." The two people on the screen went in reverse, then Foxy stopped the video at the point where the two figures appeared on the screen.

Hero pointed. "A car. Did you manage to get a plate number?"

"Nope, not yet. I'm still trying. The angle of the camera just misses it. Keep watching as I reverse the disc further."

Hero leaned in closer. "Okay, so the hooded guy got out of the vehicle and started following Daws. So, this proves the attack was intentional, yes? The question is, did the attackers know the victim, or was it just a random attack?"

"My suggestion would be if Daws was throwing his money around at the pub, these guys clocked him there and put their plan into action to rob him on the way home," Jason said.

"That's logical. Let's keep an open mind on that for now. I'll note this down on the board. Foxy, can you keep searching the discs? See if you can find the car on a different camera, where you can get a plate number. See if we can get a better shot of the driver and the person who got out of the car. It's hard to tell if we're looking at a male or female, isn't it?"

Foxy nodded. "I'm guessing the attacker was a male. My only reasoning for that is that it takes a lot of strength to strangle someone."

"Fair point in other cases perhaps. I'm undecided on this one, though. After all, Daws wasn't really in a fit state to fight off an attacker, was he?"

"There is that. Leave this with us, sir. We'll get back to you with our findings."

Hero started jotting relevant case notes on the whiteboard. "I'm surprised the house-to-house enquiries haven't stirred up any leads. Maybe we should go and check out that side of things for ourselves, Julie? What do you say?" He turned to look at his partner.

Julie stared back at him and shrugged. "Don't mind. Not a lot happening around here at the moment."

"Okay, I've got a couple of calls to make first. Why don't we have lunch then trek the streets after we've had some sustenance. I forgot to eat breakfast this morning, so I'm starving." He dug in his pocket and pulled out a coin for the vending machine.

Julie's cheeks puffed as she rose from her seat. She picked up the sandwich Jason had bought earlier and gave it to Hero when she joined him at the machine. "White coffee with one for me, sir."

"Cheeky sod." He collected his coffee and handed Julie another pound coin for her to choose her own coffee. "I'll see you in a while, after I've made my calls." In his office, he placed his cup and sandwich on the table and dialled the first person he needed to contact.

"Dog and Duck. Can I help?" Hero recognised the voice as belonging to Cathy Daws.

"Yep. The owner or manager, please?" he asked. He heard her walk away from the phone.

Soon after, a male voice answered, "Steve Gillan. What can I do for you?"

Hearing the noisy activity going on in the background, Hero said, "Hello, Mr. Gillan. Is there any chance you could take this call privately, like in an office, perhaps?"

He grunted. "I might be able to. Who wants to know?"

"Sorry, I should have introduced myself. I'm DI Nelson."

"Hold on a mo. I'll hang up and take the call out back. Two minutes."

The phone clattered, and the line went quiet. Hero was thankful the manager hadn't left the line open in case Mrs. Daws felt like listening in on their conversation.

"Right. What can I do for you, Inspector?"

"I'm dealing with a murder enquiry and following up on some information I've been given, which I'd like you to clarify, if you don't mind?"

"Murder enquiry? I'll do what I can to help."

The man's surprise left Hero wondering if Cathy Daws had confided in her boss—it certainly didn't sound that way. Why wouldn't someone inform his or her boss of a death in the family, especially if the dead person was a spouse? More to the point, he found it incredible that Cathy Daws had even shown up for her shift that day. Most people he knew would have rung in sick, understandably grief-stricken. It was all rather puzzling.

"I take it Mrs. Daws hasn't told you, then? That was Cathy who answered the phone, wasn't it?"

"That's right. What exactly is it that Cathy should have told me?" The man sounded worried.

"That her husband was killed yesterday," Hero said, shaking his head as if the man were in the room with him.

"Whoa! Seriously?" Gillan whistled.

"Seriously. We're investigating his death as murder."

"Wow, I wonder why Cathy hasn't told me?"

"Are you telling me that she's acting her normal self?" The man exhaled a large breath. "Er… yes. That is indeed what I'm saying, Inspector. Mind you, she's a tough cookie. Not exactly the cute and cuddly type. But still…"

"Well, in my experience, people deal with grief in different ways. When I visited her this morning, she seemed very concerned about money. Maybe that's why she's at work today."

"Maybe. She's always pleading poverty during her shifts. So, how can I help, Inspector?"

"The thing is, when we questioned Mrs. Daws earlier today, she said that she was at work during the time the incident occurred last night. I'm ringing up to see if that's true?"

"Hang on." Hero heard sheets of paper rustling before the man came back on the line. "Yep, looking at the rota, she was down to work last night."

"Due to work? So you can't tell me if she turned up for her shift or not?"

"Let me think. I was having drinks with some friends… was she here?" The man clicked his fingers together. "Yep, she was definitely here, because she served us with a few rounds of drinks. Now that much, I can remember."

Disappointed, Hero thanked the man for his help then hung up. Something niggling inside said he was right to have doubts about Cathy Daws's reaction, but the evidence was there—she had a cast-iron alibi that would be difficult to disprove given that there was a pub full of drinkers to corroborate her claim.

Frustrated, Hero rang the pathologist for an update. "Gerrard, it's Hero. Any news on the Daws case for me?"

"Can't talk for long, due to carry out another PM in a few minutes. I was going to ring you after that, actually. Right, here's what I've got. We found traces of cannabis in his blood."

"Interesting, well, that could throw a different light on the case if drugs are involved—a dealer wanting his money, *et cetera*."

"Yes, yes, well, that's for you to investigate. The other thing I wanted to stress to you was that in my experience, if someone is garrotted, it inevitably leads to the attack being shown as a personal one. 'In what respect?' I hear you thinking. Well again, that's down to your field of expertise to find out. All I can say is that this attack can no longer be seen as a random one."

"Interesting. Okay. Thanks, Doc. Anything else?"

"Not yet. I'll be sure to inform you when I receive all the tests back, Inspector."

After the call, Hero was deep in thought when Julie walked into the office to return his change, breaking into his trance-like state.

"Everything all right, sir?"

"Yes, thanks, Julie. I'm just going over the case in my mind. We'll eat lunch then get going, yes?"

"Whatever." His sergeant shrugged and left his office.

Before he left the station, Hero stopped off at the whiteboard to fill in the facts he'd just learned about the case. With the red marker, he circled one name several times: Cathy Daws.

It wasn't until they were underway in the car that Julie asked him why he'd done that. "I have a niggling doubt about that one. I just don't want us forgetting about her during the investigation process."

His partner shrugged again. "If she was at work, she's unlikely to have carried out the attack, though, is she?"

"Well, that's what we have to find out. Maybe she got a friend to carry out the deed for her. Have you thought of that? Let's see what the house-to-house enquiries throw up, eh?"

She turned to look out the window. "They've already come back negative," she grumbled.

"Well, it's best to check these things out, Sergeant. To my mind, at that time of night, someone should have seen, or at least heard, something. Let's hope by the time we get back, Foxy has found out more about the car and the attackers."

"We've got more chance of catching the attackers going down that route than trawling the streets." She defiantly crossed her arms.

Mindful of the burden Julie had shared with him, Hero shook his head. Any other time, he would have snapped back with a sarcastic comment, but today, he bit down hard on his tongue. He was willing to put up with her vile mood, for the time being.

As Julie predicted, the next two hours of their time turned out to be totally wasted. They jumped in the car and headed back to the station. Out of the corner of his eye, Hero noticed his partner's head moving as though she were talking to herself. Imagining the conversation going on in her head, he smirked.

Foxy couldn't cheer them up, either. Upon their return, they found all her efforts had drawn similar blanks. At six o'clock, Hero decided to call his working day to a halt and head off to the hospital.

CHAPTER FOUR

The second Hero stepped into the private room, he could tell something was wrong. Fay smiled at him, trying to disguise how upset she was. Nonetheless, he immediately saw through the façade. He squeezed her hand, and as he bent to kiss her, he noticed the damp tissue in her clenched fist. "What's wrong, love?"

She traced his face with a finger the second he sat down on the bed beside her. "It's just me being silly."

"What about?" Hero glanced over at the twins sleeping peacefully in their cots on the other side of the bed. "Anything wrong with the girls?"

"Yes," Fay said before she broke down in tears.

"Fay, love, you're worrying me. Please tell me what's wrong."

A nurse entered the room before Fay could explain. "Come on, Mrs. Nelson, Fay, it's not as bad as all that."

"What isn't? Will someone please tell me what the hell is going on?"

Fay glanced up and pleaded with the nurse to assist her.

"Nurse? Someone? Anyone?" Hero asked, his gaze moving between his wife and the nurse.

"All right. Upon further examination of the twins, we found a slight problem with Zara."

"Problem? What sort of problem?" Hero shot off the bed and ran to the side of the cot to check his children.

"It's really nothing to worry about. Zara has a hernia. A Diaphragmatic hernia. It's a slight birth defect, which means there's an abnormal opening in the diaphragm, the muscle that helps her breathe."

Hero was amazed by the nurse's calmness. "That sounds a big deal to me, nurse."

"Really, it isn't. If you need the doctor to reassure you, I can page him?"

"So, what does it mean?" Hero's legs began to shake.

"Your daughter is booked in for surgery tomorrow. Honestly, there really isn't anything to worry about. It occurs in one in every twenty-two hundred to five thousand births. We need to place the internal organs in the right place and stitch up the opening. Zara currently has a slight breathing problem, which will be cured once she's had the operation."

"If you're sure. Could it be anything else?"

The nurse shook her head. "No. Stop worrying. We know exactly what the cause is, and we're going to fix it tomorrow. You'll see. She'll be fine after the operation."

"Isn't she young to be having an op?"

"Yes, but it's a necessary operation. She'll pull through it. Look at it this way—if we don't carry out the operation, Zara will be far worse off." The nurse walked around the bed and stood beside him, rubbing his back to comfort him.

Hero looked up at her with moist eyes. She smiled and nodded.

Fay patted the bed beside her, beckoning him to sit. "We must be strong, Hero. It's for the best. Ignore me. My hormones are still out of kilter because of the birth. The doctor assured me that the operation will make Zara's life better, and that's all that matters in the end, isn't it?"

He hugged her tight and kissed her on the lips. "Let's hope she has enough fight in her to pull through the op then."

"She has. She's her father's daughter, after all. If there were any doubts, I wouldn't let them go ahead. You know that, right?"

"Yeah, I know, love. It won't stop me worrying about it, though. What type of father would I be if I didn't worry?"

"The type I wouldn't want to share my life with. Zara will be fine. We'll all be fine. Gosh, the sooner we can get out of here, the better. I miss you and Louie. How is he?"

Hero recognised an attempted distraction when he heard one. "I spoke to your mum this morning. He got off to school all right. I can't wait to have you all back at home with me. The house feels so empty—I feel empty—without you all there with me."

"You're so sweet. Let's get this operation out of the way first. Providing that goes well, we should be home in a few days. Shouldn't we, nurse?"

Hero had been so caught up in his emotions that he'd totally forgotten the nurse was in the same room. He gave her an embarrassed smile.

"Yep, there's no reason at all why the girls shouldn't be at home with you within a few days. Please, don't worry about the operation, okay?"

Hero and Fay nodded, and the nurse left the room. They held each other tightly and looked over at their baby girls, who were sleeping as if they didn't have a care in the world.

He stayed at the hospital for another hour before Fay urged him to go home and rest. She too looked exhausted from the day's emotional downturn. Hero arrived home around nine and went straight to bed, where he dreamt about his girls running rings around Louie and him.

* * *

The following morning, Hero had not been in the office long when he took a phone call from Superintendent Cranwell's secretary, who asked Hero to join Cranwell in his office as soon as possible.

With trepidation twisting his empty stomach inside out, he walked along the narrow corridor to the super's office. As he pushed open the outer office door, the super's friendly personal assistant, Sandra, greeted him. "Is it all right if I go through?" he asked.

"Of course, he's expecting you. Oh, congratulations, by the way. Double the trouble, eh?"

Hero's eyes rolled up to the ceiling, and he grinned. "Yeah, thanks, Sandra. We'll soon see just how much trouble when they're all settled at home."

"You'll be fine. At least your wife will be."

Hero knocked on the door before he pushed it open. Superintendent Cranwell was on the phone, so Hero hesitated until Cranwell motioned for Hero to join him.

Finishing his call, the super reached across the table to shake Hero's hand. The gesture was unusual in itself; usually, he greeted Hero with a brief nod before getting down to business. "Congratulations, son. How are they all?"

"Thanks, sir. Well, I guess the answer should be they're all fit and well, except they're not."

The super leaned back in his chair and intertwined his fingers across his slim stomach. A concerned frown replaced the smile on his face. "Meaning?"

"One of the twins has to have an emergency op today. She has a hernia. I've been assured that she will be all right, but it won't stop me from worrying about her."

"Oh, dear, that's a shame. Right, I suppose you're wondering why I called you in to see me?" the super asked, swiftly changing the subject.

"Yes, sir. Nothing wrong, is there?"

"Nothing at all, which is remarkable as far as you're concerned, given your errant past." He laughed as Hero's face dropped. "I jest, of course. Anyway, I wanted to know what your plans are?"

"Plans? In respect to what, sir?"

"Your paternity leave. You're entitled to it, you know?"

"I am? I've never even thought about it, what with being new to this fatherhood lark."

"Well, I suggest you do think about it. What cases are you working at the moment? There's never a good time to take time off. On the other hand, if your schedule isn't too chocker right now, it might be something for you to consider."

Hero thought over the case he'd just taken on and had barely had the time to sink his teeth into. "Maybe I could take a week off after I've wrapped up the case I'm overseeing. What with the operation…"

The super sprang forward and placed his hands flat on the desk. "Operation?"

Hero tried hard not to shake his head in disbelief. He was used to his superior always thinking ahead to his next sentence and disregarding a person's response. He obviously hadn't heard Hero mention the operation the first time. "Yes, one of the girls has a hernia. She's booked in for an emergency op today, sir."

"Goodness, man, what the heck are you doing at work?"

Hero smiled briefly. "It's fine, sir. I'd rather be at work than pacing up and down a hospital corridor for hours. Fay insisted I concentrate on the job, too. She's worrying enough for both of us." He chuckled, trying to end his sentence on a light-hearted note.

"Do I have to order you to take time off, Nelson?"

"Sir, honestly, I'd rather just get on with my job. How about if I say once this case is finished, I'll definitely take time off? Will that make you happy?"

"Very well. In the meantime, if the little ones need you, then don't hesitate to take the time off, all right? We're not all callous bastards in the Met. I'm a father, too, and I know when my kids are ill, it tugs at my heartstrings." He looked down at the portrait of his family and smiled. "It gets tougher as they get older, you know?"

"Yes, sir, so I've been led to believe. Was there anything else? I don't want to appear rude, but I'd like to chase up a few enquiries to the case, if that's all right?"

"Of course, don't let me hold you up. What's your gut feeling about the case?"

"My gut is screaming out the wife is involved. However, her alibi is making me doubt my instincts. We've got some valuable CCTV footage we're investigating, which leads us to believe that two people were at the scene. Involved or otherwise, that's what we're trying to figure out. The pathologist says everything indicates to the victim knowing his attacker. It's just putting all the pieces together that's going to be the hard part."

"I have confidence in you and your team to pull it off. Hey, what's the frown for? Have you got a problem with a team member?"

"Not really a problem per se, but Julie Shaw's mum has terminal cancer. I'm not saying it's affecting her work. Nevertheless, I do think she'll be needing time off soon as her mum has now been admitted to hospice."

"Right, I'm sorry to hear that. Keep an eye on the situation, and if you need to replace her for any length of time, let me know."

"Yes, sir." Hero rose from his seat and left the office.

Back in the incident room, he did the rounds with the team, asking if they had any new leads since the previous night. He started with Lance. "How did it go last night at the pub?"

"Not so good, sir. I managed to locate and chat with the two men. But they were lukewarm, not exactly brimming with pleasure to be seen with me. And yes, I did ask them discreetly, as you instructed."

"All right. What did you pick up from them in that case? You know, any gut reaction to either man? Do you think they knew more about the incident than they were letting on?"

"Nothing, sir. Like I said, it was akin to getting blood out of a stone. A few grunts and nods to any questions I asked. If I had to place a bet if either man was involved in the attack, I'd say Stan Foster was a likely candidate."

"Okay, let's get a thorough check going on him." Hero patted Lance on the shoulder. "Good work."

He moved on to sit on the edge of Foxy's desk. "Anything else turn up in the footage, Foxy?"

"I'll get back on to it today, sir. I'm taking my time, searching frame by frame to see what I can find. That's going to hamper things a little. Sorry."

"Nope, that's exactly what I'd expect of you, Foxy. Carry on. Let me know what you find out."

"Yes, sir."

Julie had her head buried in paperwork when Hero approached. "Everything all right, Julie?"

When she glanced up, Hero could tell, by the redness of her eyes, that she'd been crying. "Yes, sir."

Hero knew the opposite was true. "Okay, my door is open if you need a chat."

Julie nodded and looked down at the paperwork again as if to dismiss him.

"Can you do me a favour, Julie?"

"Okay, what do you need?"

"I *was* going to ask Foxy. The thing is, I'd rather she concentrated all of her efforts on the CCTV at the moment. Can you dig really deep into Cathy Daws's past for me? Lance is doing the same with Stan Foster. Let's see what we can find out about those two, yes?"

"You think they're in cahoots?"

"We've got nothing else to go on. They both had a connection with the victim. Let's see where it leads."

"Okay, I'll get back to you within the hour," Julie told him.

"Thanks. I'll be in my office, dealing with the usual mundane paperwork."

On his way to his office, he changed direction and headed for the whiteboard. He shook his head, frustrated that he couldn't add anything else to the nearly blank board. His gaze hooked onto Cathy Daws's name. He heard a phone ring in the incident room, and Julie answered it.

"Sir?"

He spun around to face her. She held the phone out for him to take the call.

"DI Nelson. How can I help?"

"Get off my back. You're barking up the wrong tree."

"Who is this?" Hero could tell that the male caller was covering the phone with something in the hope of disguising his voice, which was ridiculous. The caller's identity was obvious, since the team had spoken only to a few possible suspects so far.

The caller continued with his nonsensical call. "It doesn't matter who it is. This is your one and only warning. You hear me?"

"Hang on a minute. You're telling me to back off, but you won't tell me who you are. Plus, it sounds like you're issuing me with a threat, am I right?"

The man groaned on the end of the phone.

Hero held back a chuckle then picked a name to try. "Mr. Foster? I'm right, aren't I?"

The line went dead. Hero clicked his fingers and pointed at Jason. "Jase, you and Lance get over to Foster's flat and pick him up. Lance, have you managed to find out the man's address yet?"

"Not yet, sir. I'll get on it right away."

"Hurry up, man. I want him pulled in for questioning. No bugger threatens me and gets away with it."

Julie cleared her throat with a dainty cough. "Are you sure it was him, sir?"

"I'm sure, Julie. Are you doubting my instincts?"

"No, sir."

Hero stormed over to Lance's desk and fiddled with his computer mouse. "Here, that's what you need. Now get over there. I want you back with him within the next thirty minutes."

Lance shifted his heavy frame out of the chair and followed Jason out of the incident room. Hero shook his head. *Sometimes, just sometimes, I think that man is on a different planet from the rest of us.*

He finally made it into his office but found it difficult to concentrate. *Maybe I should have picked the bugger up myself!*

Half an hour later, Jason knocked on Hero's door and poked his head around the doorframe. "Sorry, gov. He wasn't there."

"What?" Hero threw his pen, and it skidded across the desk. "Damn. Did you knock on the neighbour's door to see if he'd been around?"

"Yes, boss. They haven't seen him since yesterday."

"Very well. There's nothing we can do. Wait—yes there is! Get on to the control room and ask them to keep an eye out for either Foster or his car. He does have a vehicle, doesn't he? My betting is that it's the same vehicle we spotted on the CCTV camera, despite what he said about me barking up the wrong tree during the phone call. Once a criminal, always a criminal, in my book."

"I'll get on to it now, sir."

A brainwave struck Hero, he reached for the phone and dialled his journalist friend. "Dave? Yeah, it's Hero. Have you got time for a quick chat?"

"Hi, sure. I've always got time for a mate. Is it about a case?"

"It is. Fancy meeting me at the pub at lunchtime?"

"Name the pub, and I'll be there."

"Dog and Duck. Do you know it?"

"Yep, what time?" Dave asked.

"About one?"

"Yep. See you then."

Hero met his good friend in the car park, and together, they entered the dingy public house. Cathy Daws's face dropped when Hero walked in and headed her way.

"What are you having, Dave?"

"Pint of bitter, mate. What's all this about?"

Hero winked at him and turned his attention to Cathy Daws. "Pint of bitter and a glass of Coke, the full-fat variety, please?" Then he turned to Dave. "I wanted to discuss a case I'm working on." He looked over his shoulder to see if Cathy was listening to their conversation. She obviously was, so he added, "Let's talk about it more when we get a table, eh, mate?"

"Okay. How's the family? Are they still in hospital?" Dave asked innocently enough.

Hero cringed. He really didn't want to discuss his personal life in front of someone he suspected of being involved in a violent crime. "Yeah, not bad. How's work? Still struggling to meet the daily deadline target?"

Cathy Daws banged down two glasses on the bar, making Hero jump. "That'll be four pounds fifty."

Hero paid the woman, picked up the glasses, and chose a table far enough away from the bar to ensure that Daws wouldn't overhear their conversation.

"Why all the secrecy?" Dave asked, leaning across the table.

"We're investigating the death of that woman's husband," Hero whispered back.

Dave glanced at the woman. "You're kidding me?"

"Don't bloody look at her, you idiot."

Dave turned back to face him. "So, when did her husband die?"

"A few days ago. Looks upset, don't she?" Hero's question was laced with sarcasm.

"Hmm... not really. How did he die?"

Hero twisted in his seat, just in case Daws turned out to be a lip-reader. "Murdered. Someone garrotted him in an alley."

"Not your run-of-the-mill mugging then?"

"Nope. I wanted to meet up because this guy is a petty criminal. At least he has been in the past. And yes, before you say it, it grieves me to waste so much time on such a dipshit, but a murder is a murder, right? Anyway, I wondered if any of your snouts could shed some light on the victim?"

"I can ask. God, you get all the sweet jobs, don't you?"

Hero tutted and took a sip of his ice-cold Coke. "The thing is, I'm sure the wife is involved in this somehow, despite her giving us a decent alibi."

"Alibi?"

"Yeah, she was working here at the time he was killed. Pretty tight, that one."

"All right, it doesn't mean that she hasn't paid anyone to bump him off, though."

Hero shook his head. "Paid with what? I've seen her gaff, mate. Believe me when I say she's as broke as they come. She did let it slip that her husband had stolen the housekeeping money on the day of his death. He was intoxicated when he was murdered, so we can safely assume that he got rat-arsed with her money. I'd hardly think that was a motive for his murder."

Dave sniggered. "Okay, I shouldn't laugh. It's very odd that she's at work, though, so soon after his death."

"That's what I thought, too. Anyway, we're obviously running the usual background checks on both the husband and the wife, but if you can ask around for me, that'd be great?"

"I'll see what I can do." He took out his reporter's notebook and jotted down the names.

"Add this one to your list. Stan Foster, friend of the deceased. Apparently, he was drinking with him a few hours before Daws died. I received a threatening call, I suspect from Foster, telling me to back off. I sent two officers around to pick him up and bring him in for questioning, but he'd gone AWOL."

"Same kind of thing, petty criminal, yes?"

"Yep. There's one other thing to consider when you're questioning the snouts. A drug element. Daws had cannabis in him. We're thinking that possibly a gang dealing in drugs might have killed him. Pure conjecture, of course, but if you're asking the questions anyway, you might as well put that one around, too."

"Right. I'll get on to this when I return to the office. Ring me if you think of anything else, okay?"

"Things are a little thin on the ground at present, mate. The term 'clutching at straws' comes to mind, until something else crops up. As quick as you can with the info. I'd appreciate it."

Both men finished their drinks and left the pub. As he shut the door, Hero looked behind him, and sure enough, Cathy Daws was glaring at him through narrowed eyes. Feeling devilish, he wiggled his fingers and smiled broadly at her, much to her annoyance.

CHAPTER FIVE

The incident room was busy with chatter when Hero returned to the station. "What's going on?" he demanded with a frown.

"A body has been found under a railway bridge, sir," Jason told him.

"On our patch?"

"Yes, sir."

"Right, get me the details. Julie, are you ready to go?" His partner glanced up at him, and he saw immediately that she'd been crying again. "Would you rather I took someone else with me?" he asked as he walked over to her desk.

She nodded and swallowed hard. "If you don't mind, sir."

"Go home, eh?"

"I couldn't do that. Foxy can go with you. I can take over her job with the CCTV discs."

"Did you manage to find out anything about Cathy Daws while I was out?" She lifted her notebook and handed it to him. The answer stared back at him from the two lines she'd written: nothing much. "Great, well, there's little we can do about that, is there? Okay, if you're sure you want to sit this one out and stick around here, I'll take Foxy with me."

"It's about time she started using her talents more out in the field."

"If everything gets on top of you, you have my permission to go home, all right?"

"Yes, sir, thank you."

Hero nodded then marched across the room to Foxy. "Grab your jacket. You're coming with me, Foxy lady." He stopped dead and turned to give her an embarrassed smile. "Er… that kind of came out the wrong way."

As though the comment had passed her by, Foxy rose from the chair with a look of confusion covering her face. "I am? What about this lot?" She swept her hand over the discs scattered across her desk.

"It's all in hand. Julie's going to take care of that while we're out."

Foxy looked over at Julie, who nodded her acceptance of the situation. "I'm good to go then, sir."

"Right. Let's get out of here." Hero strode past Jason, grabbed the piece of paper the young detective was holding out to him, and left the incident room with Foxy trotting behind him.

Once in the car, Hero programed the location into his sat nav and headed off. Foxy struck up a conversation, and Hero could hear in her voice how nervous she was.

"Hey, you'll be fine. Stop fretting. How's that hubby of yours doing in Vice? Is promotion on the cards for him yet?" Hero knew how much Sally loved talking about her husband and how proud Frank was of his work with the unit. As far as Hero was concerned, Frank was welcome to it, Hero had never considered joining Vice in the past, and he couldn't envision joining in the foreseeable future, either. He couldn't imagine dealing with the dregs and scum of Manchester every day. His last case had put him in direct contact with some treacherous people, and he'd found himself slap-bang in the middle of a gang war that had forced him to investigate several crimes in a notorious police no-go area. His nerves had jangled constantly during that case. He definitely couldn't live with shredded nerves on a daily basis the way Frank had to.

"Yes, it looks like they want him to start climbing the ladder. It's his call. I think he likes being involved at 'ground level,' if you like. Not sure he could hack being stuck in the station all day, buried under a mountain of paperwork. It's something he needs to consider carefully over the next few weeks."

"I'm sure he'll make the right decision in the long run, for both of you." He steered the car slowly down the narrow lane that led to the crime scene. Several cars blocked the way, and two uniformed officers were standing behind the crime scene tape. Hero parked the car behind all the others, and the two detectives stepped out of the vehicle. Hero flashed his warrant card, then both he and Foxy ducked under the tape and headed down the muddy bank towards the Scene of Crime Officers already working the area.

"Are you all right? Probably not the best footwear to have chosen." Hero pointed at Foxy's three-inch heels.

"I'll be fine. I can clean them up when I get back to the office. I really wasn't expecting to be out in the field today, sir."

"Sorry, I suppose I should've checked before volunteering you for the role. Okay, let's see what we have. Ah... I see a familiar face."

Hero entered the tunnel and walked up to a man wearing a protective white paper suit. "Hello, Gerrard. What do we have?"

"A dog walker found the body, or rather his dog did. It's not pretty. Looks like the corpse has been here for somewhere between two and three weeks. Heavily decomposed. I think the strays have been feeding off his face and hands because there's very little left."

Both men turned when Foxy gulped and her face went a mild shade of green. "You all right, Sally?"

She nodded. "I'll be fine in a minute, sir. It's the smell..." With that, she hurled against the tunnel wall. Luckily she'd had the sense to change direction in time so as not to contaminate the crime scene.

Hero and Gerrard smirked and moved towards the body. They crouched as Gerrard continued his briefing, revealing what he'd discovered about the body so far.

"I'm estimating the man is in his mid-twenties to early thirties. He probably died from the wound to his throat. It was a vicious attack—his head was virtually severed."

"An intentional attack full of rage for the victim, in that case?" Hero suggested.

"Looks that way, although I'll be more definite once we're back at the mortuary. You can see that he suffered numerous wounds to the chest area, presumably with a knife of sorts. So either one of them could have been the fatal wound."

"Is there enough of him left to get an ID? Have you found any ID? I suppose I should have asked that first."

Gerrard shook his head. "Nothing as yet. Maybe the killer wanted us to believe it was some kind of mugging, but the ferociousness of the attack leads me to think otherwise."

"Why here? I'm inclined to believe you're right in that he was probably, or *unfortunately* I should say, led here with one thing in mind. Have your guys found a possible vehicle anywhere nearby?"

"Another negative. That doesn't mean to say he didn't have one when he arrived. The killer could have stolen it, or the victim might have parked his car a few streets away and arrived on foot. Once we can get him identified, you can start searching for the vehicle."

Gerrard stood up.

Hero remained crouching and scanned the area around the body. But he came up blank. "You don't think he was killed somewhere else and dumped here, do you?" he asked Gerrard as he stood up.

"No, I don't think so. There's a lot of blood pooling, and"—he held out his hand to one of his team for a torch—"there's a lot of blood spatter on the walls. Of course, we'll have to analyse the blood to see if it came from the victim, but the likelihood in this case is there for all to see, I believe."

Gerrard moved to where the victim's head pointed north, then he made a stabbing motion. He was right—if the murderer had been standing in that same position when he attacked the victim and the victim fell on the spot, then, yes, the victim's blood could have easily splayed across the wall behind them, to form the pattern on the bricks.

"I see. If there are no fingerprints to help with identification, is there any way we can maybe get one of those clay models made up of his face?" Hero bent down and studied the face. "The bone structure is all there. It's just the skin that's missing. How about it?"

"I can certainly have a word with a colleague of mine specialising in the forensic sculpture field. Depending on her workload, I can't see why we shouldn't be able to sort that out, Hero."

"That's great. The sooner we can obtain some features or a face, the quicker we can get the word out in the media. Get back to me today about that, will you, Gerrard?"

Gerrard shook his head and tutted. "I'll do my best. I'm not going to make promises I can't keep. As you can see I'll be a little preoccupied first thing."

Hero shrugged innocently and joked, "You will? Can't imagine what you'll be up to. Right, I better get out of here while my scalp is still intact. Anything else I should know before I leave?"

"No, I think we've covered everything. I'll make the necessary calls and get on with the examination first thing. Do you want to observe?"

"Do you need me to be there? I'm still three feet deep in another case right now."

Gerrard shook his head. "No, you don't need to attend. I'll get back to you later with my conclusions."

When they were back in the car, Hero asked Foxy, "How are you feeling now? Had I known you had a queasy stomach, I would have asked one of the boys to join me. Sorry about that."

"There's no need to be sorry, sir. It was a bit of a shock to me. That's all. Stupid, really, considering I spend half my days looking at gruesome photos and never have a problem. Yet when I'm called to attend a scene, the first thing I do is spill my guts. Hardly professional, is it?"

He laughed. "Don't feel bad. It happens to us all on the first case."

She turned sharply to face him. "You? It happened to you, too?"

"Yep, and ninety-nine percent of the force, I suspect, if they dare to admit it. It's not so much the sight of seeing a dead body that upsets the stomach. It's the vile smell. That one back there was a particularly nasty one, I have to say."

"Then why didn't it affect you, sir?" Foxy asked, a perplexed look creasing her brow.

Hero pulled a small pot of Vicks out of his jacket pocket and handed it to her. "Meet your new best friend."

"Vicks! I don't get it, sir."

"Call it a trick of the trade. Most coppers apply a little under their noses when they either show up at a bad scene, such as that one, or when they have to sit in on a post mortem."

"Come to think of it, I remember seeing something about using this as a barrier in one of those autopsy programmes on the crime channel," she admitted.

"You live and learn, Foxy, every day in this job, so it would seem."

"I guess I have a long learning curve ahead of me, if that's the case," she said quietly, leaning her head against the headrest.

"When we get back, I want you to chase up the address of the dog owner who reported the crime. We'll call and see him this afternoon, if he's free."

"Yes, sir."

Once Foxy had tracked down the man's address, they set off again. Hero was pleased to see that the colour had returned to his temporary partner's cheeks. They pulled up outside what appeared to be a warden-protected block of flats for the elderly.

Mr. Mitchell was eager to see them and made a point of introducing the two detectives to his little beagle, which had dragged him to the body of the victim. "He's the hero in all this. Jackson led me to the body, not a pretty sight. Have you seen it? Turned my stomach upside down and put me off my tomato soup. I always have tomato soup for lunch, I do."

Hero smiled at the wizened old man and patted the dog, which had propped himself up against Hero's leg.

"Do you often go down that way to walk Jackson?" Hearing his name, the dog turned to look at Hero. He stroked its head and glanced up at the dog's owner for a response.

"Now and again. Haven't been down there for a few days—maybe it's weeks. I can't be sure, really."

"Any reason for you changing your routine?" Hero asked, thinking the man might have stumbled across an altercation or witnessed something untoward and been afraid to get involved.

"The weather mainly. When it's wet, it gets terribly muddy down there, like today. I hadn't anticipated that today, any of it."

"I see. Can you remember when you last visited the area?"

The man tapped the side of his nose with a finger. "Ah… I see where you're going with this. You're trying to find out how long the body has been down there, ain't ya? I've seen enough of them CSI programmes on the TV to understand what you're getting at."

Hero smiled at the man and stroked the dog again. "There's no fooling you, Mr. Mitchell. I was also asking if you'd seen anything out of the ordinary. Anyone you perceived to be up to no good, perhaps?"

The man's mouth twisted as he thought. "Nothing that I can think of. I'm sorry. I'd tell you if I had. I haven't been around that area for at least three weeks, if that helps. I've not been too steady on my feet of late, to be honest, so Jackson there has been neglected for a couple of weeks. He's a good dog, doesn't bother me at all, as though he senses when I'm not so well."

"Dogs have a knack of picking up on things like that, it's true. Oh well, if you can't tell us anything else, we better get off and leave you to it." Hero stood up and walked towards the front door.

Mr. Mitchell held out a hand for Hero to shake. "I'm sorry I couldn't tell you more, son. I hope you catch the bastard who did it. No one deserves to get done over like that. Horrible business." His final words were attached to a shudder.

"Thanks, Mr. Mitchell. Take care of yourself and little Jackson over there."

"I will. He's all I've got in this world," the man said sadly, eyeing the dog standing next to the living room door.

When she got back in the car, Foxy pulled the seatbelt around her and said, "That must have shaken him up, finding the body like that. Poor bloke."

"Yeah, there are some things in this life that folks should never be allowed to see, and that's one of them. Let's see what everyone's been up to back at the station, and then I think we'll call it a day. I don't know about you, but I've seen enough and had enough excitement for one day."

"Yeah, me, too. God knows what we'll be eating for dinner tonight. Not sure my stomach's up to much."

"These things are sent to try us, Foxy. You know that, right?"

* * *

"Okay, what do we have?" Hero asked the second he and Foxy arrived in the incident room. He made his way over to the blank whiteboard, not the one they'd started for Stuart Daws's murder, and began writing out the details of the second crime.

His team brought their notebooks and settled into the seats nearest the boards.

Lance spoke first. "Regarding the other case, sir, I looked into this guy Foster's past. Actually, I'm still finding some snippets out about him."

"And, Lance?"

"Well, it'll be no surprise to you that, yes, he drives a similar model car to the one seen on the CCTV footage. He's been in and out of nick for the past twenty-odd years, since he was nineteen."

"For what?"

"Anything and everything, really. Petty stuff, that is, nothing too heavy. I suppose the heaviest charge is actual bodily harm. He's into drugs, burglary. To me, he's been let off lightly by certain judges over the years, only carrying out community service in a few cases. Not sure what kind of deterrent the judges thought they'd be, especially for a reoffender."

"Shit happens, Lance. Trouble is, the judges are being told to stop sending people to prison for minor offences because the prisons are all pretty much full. I know it isn't right, but..."

"Yes, sir." Lance nodded reluctantly.

"Have we got a licence number for his car?"

"Yep, I've put out an alert for it already, sir. Considering he's gone missing, he's obviously got something to hide," Lance informed him.

"That's my take on it. Julie, any advancement on the CCTV footage? Can we match the plate to Foster's yet?"

"Not that I can see, no. Disappointingly, there's nothing more on the footage to help us as yet, sir. Maybe we should just concentrate on tracking down Foster, bring him in for questioning, and go from there?"

"Thanks, Julie. I think we've already established that should be how we proceed," Hero shot back at her, instantly regretting his harsh tone. He tried to offer a brief smile as an apology, but his partner just returned a blank gaze. "Right, this is what Foxy and I uncovered about the new case. It's basic at the moment, until the PM has been carried out. The man, in his late twenties to early thirties, had his throat slit. Not just that—his attacker almost severed his head from his body during the frenzied attack. The victim's body was found by a man walking his dog. The pathologist reckons we're looking at the corpse being at least two to three weeks old. The dog walker believes it has been three weeks since he walked his dog down there because of the poor weather, so that would definitely match up to the pathologist's speculation. Not only was the victim strangled, but he was also attacked with a sharp object—in all probability, a knife—and stabbed numerous times in the chest."

"So he saw his attacker then, sir?" Jason asked.

"It looks that way, Jason. I've asked the pathologist to get a forensic sculpture to make up a face for us. As soon as we have that, we can try and make a formal identification, either through the system or via the media. Actually, first thing—Foxy, can you organise a press conference for in a few days? We'll need to put out a request for information if anyone saw anything suspicious in the area."

"Will do, sir. I'll jot down all the relevant information we have in readiness for the conference, if you like?"

"That'll be great, Foxy. I'll keep on top of the pathologist to see if any other evidence comes to light during the examination. Or if the victim has any tell-tale birthmarks *et cetera,* we can pass that on to the public. Okay, if that's everything, I suggest we call it a day and start again afresh tomorrow."

The team agreed in unison, and Hero headed into his office to tidy up his desk before leaving the station. He intended to drop in on Fay on his way home. He rang the hospital and asked to be put through to his wife's room.

"Hello?"

"Hi, Fay. I'm on my way. Do you need anything brought in?"

"Hero, aren't you going to ask how the operation went?"

He kicked himself under the table for being so preoccupied with work that he'd totally forgotten about the scheduled op that afternoon. He tried to bluff his way out. "Of course I was. I just thought I'd see if you wanted anything first. How did it go?"

"Hmm…" Fay said dubiously. "It went fine. I can breathe properly again. I mean, *we* can breathe easily again."

"That's great, darling. I'll be with you in half an hour."

"Can't wait to see you."

Hero arrived at the hospital, kissed Fay, then went over to Zoe, sleeping in her cot. "Where's Zara? In recovery?"

"Yes, they want to keep an eye on her overnight to make sure there are no side effects to the op. The doctor reassured me that it was a total success. She should lead a normal, perfect life from now on."

He sat on the bed beside her. "That's great, hon. Any news on when you'll be free to come home?" Hero leaned forward and gave her a kiss that took his wife's breath away.

"Either tomorrow or the next day, hopefully. Hey, you can forget about having any sex for a good few weeks yet. It takes a lot of effort to produce two kids at once, you know, and the doc recommends abstinence for at least six weeks."

He winked at her. "The thought never crossed my mind, honest. Is your mum still all right looking after Louie?"

"She's loving it, and he's revelling in the fact that Mum is eager to fuss over him, too."

"I'm pretty busy working a case, two cases, at the moment, but I'll stop at the supermarket on the way home if you want me to get anything specific, like nappies."

Fay touched his face. "You're sweet. Thanks for thinking of that, hon, but I stocked up on supplies before the babies came. Have you heard how Cara is getting on with her training?"

"Yeah, she rang up the other night to bitch about the brain-dead recruits in her group. The thing is, she's just too brainy for some people to handle. If she can make it through the training, keep a tight rein on that loose tongue of hers, and not fly off the handle at the slightest thing, she'll prove an asset to the force. It's a big *if*, though."

"Is there any chance she'll become part of your team once she's finished her training?"

Hero shook his head. "I wouldn't have thought so. She'll have to spend some time in uniform first. It's up to her to show an aptitude for the job before any promotions come her way. Like I said, that depends on whether she can keep her mouth shut."

"She'll learn to keep her mouth shut, under your guidance. I can also see her being a great success and a valued member of anyone's team. I bet she's more reliable than most of the applicants the Met signs up," Fay said, smiling at him.

"Yeah, but you know as well as I do that once she gets a bee in her bonnet about something, she'll latch on to it until that problem is dealt with in a satisfactory manner. To her satisfaction, that is."

"She'll be fine. It shows she has initiative and is eager to right all that's wrong in this world. We'll give her all the support she needs anyway, yes?"

"Oh, I intend to. It'll just be an added burden to my already-fraught life."

"You poor thing. Give me a kiss and then go home and get some rest. Are you eating properly?"

Hero kissed Fay and his daughter before he responded. "Yes, dear. I've pulled a few of the plated meals out of the freezer as per your instructions."

"Good, glad to hear it."

"I'll drop in tomorrow after work, unless you get the all-clear to leave the hospital early. Ring me if they kick you out of here, yes?"

"I will. Sleep well."

CHAPTER SIX

Both cases dragged on until the following Monday, when Gerrard Brown telephoned Hero with his conclusions from the post mortem and the ensuing results from the victim whose body was found in the tunnel.

"Gerrard, you beat me to it. I was going to give you a prod this afternoon," Hero joked.

"Ha, you won't be joking when you hear what I have to say. Would you like to do it over the phone, or do you want to do it in person?"

"Sounds ominous? I'll come down there. I could do with a break from the office. Put the kettle on. I'll be there in ten minutes."

"Sure, I think it's for the best."

Hero swept through the incident room and called over his shoulder, "Off to get the path results. Be back soon."

The wipers scraped across the windscreen on the journey over to the mortuary. Hero parked the car and ran inside the building before rain poured down from the threatening black clouds overhead. He ran down the steps to the lower level and pushed open the door. Gerrard was waiting for him in the corridor.

They shook hands before entering Gerrard's office. Two steaming cups of coffee sat on the heavily laden desk. "I thought *my* desk was bad."

Gerrard tutted. "Paperwork is near enough sixty percent of our job now. Bloody pain in the arse, and most of it is unnecessarily repeated. Anyway, let's see what we have." He opened a file and handed Hero a ten-by-eight glossy photo.

"Wow, that's superb. If we don't manage to identify the victim from that, then we never will. I'm impressed."

"You should be. Jackie does exceptional work. I've never had a single one of her sculptures that has failed to garner an identification of a victim."

"I can believe it. I'll run it through the system when I return to the office. Anything else?"

"Of course. There were no great surprises after I carried out the PM. What I told you at the scene still stands. The injury to the neck was definitely the fatal blow."

"Okay, fair enough. What are you holding back, Gerrard?" Hero raised an eyebrow.

He pulled another manila folder from his pile and placed it on his desk, alongside the other one in front of him. When he glanced up at Hero again, he was suppressing a gleeful expression. "One of your cases, the John Doe yet to be identified." He pushed the file forward then tapped his hand on the other file. "And then we have this file, which belongs to the victim I carried out a PM on last week, another of your cases, I believe."

"Stop beefing up your part, Gerrard. This other victim wouldn't be Stuart Daws, would it?"

The pathologist winked at Hero and pointed at him. "Bang on."

"So, what's the connection? The cause of death? Nope, it can't be that, because Daws was strangled, garrotted. What am I missing?"

"Okay, here are the comparisons I found. Both had neck injuries. Both victims had cannabis in their system—"

"As well as half the people in the UK, I shouldn't wonder. Go on?"

"Fibres."

"What sort of fibres?"

"The victim in the tunnel had several coloured synthetic fibres attached to his pullover."

"Right, I'm presuming those fibres match the pullover or some form of clothing Daws was wearing. Am I right?"

"Spot on."

"Well, well, well. So is it safe to assume that Daws carried out the murder, then?"

"We've got a long way to go before we can confirm that, but my ultimate assumption would be if he didn't kill the John Doe, he was certainly at the scene of the murder. One final comparison is that we found traces of the John Doe's skin under Stuart Daws's fingernails."

Hero rested his elbow on the table and placed his fist under his chin. "Hmm… well, that's a very interesting outcome indeed. The question is, what motive are we looking at?"

"That's your department, not mine."

"Well, there's one good thing to come of this."

"What's that?" Gerrard frowned.

"At least I don't have to split my team up. If the crimes are linked, then there's a good chance we can wrap this case up quicker than if we were classing them as two separate investigations. If you get where I'm coming from?"

"I do. I have to get on with another examination now." He chuckled briefly. "At least there's no chance of this case being added to your growing list of victims. This one died in an old folk's home."

Hero nodded but didn't join in with the pathologist's light-heartedness about his next PM. Hero headed back to the station. His mind was working overtime during the course of the drive, so much that he almost ran into the vehicle in front of him when the car stopped short because a dog ran into the road.

After successfully making it to the station in one piece, he bolted up the stairs two at a time and barged through the incident room door. "We've got a great picture of the John Doe," he announced. "The priority is to put a name to the face. Plus, we have a connection between the two cases." Hero walked over to the evidence board and picked up the marker. First, he added to the board the information on the John Doe case that tied the victim to Stuart Daws. Then he drew a series of lines linking the names together with the DNA evidence the pathologist had just given him.

Julie stood next to him. "So, by that, I take it we can assume that Daws killed the John Doe?"

"That's my line of thinking, Julie, yes."

"Okay, do you want me to look into Daws's background and pull out some names? Was the victim a likely friend at one point, do you think?"

"Maybe. I'm still inclined to go down the drugs route on this one. Plus, there's the small matter that I don't trust the wife, either. See what you can find out."

"Do you want me to see if we can utilise the media to get a probable identification?"

"You get on to the TV, and I'll ring Dave Wheeler, see if his paper can run the picture this evening for us. That should set the phones ringing, hopefully."

Julie rushed back to her desk and picked up the phone. Hero finished off writing up the details and went through to his office to ring his journalist friend.

"Dave, it's Hero. I don't suppose you've found out anything yet?"

"No, I was going to get back to you later today. The information is coming back slower than a wizened old granny crossing the road."

Hero snorted at the image Dave's words conjured up. "That's a shame. I've just come back from the pathology lab. Looks like we've got two victims. A John Doe whose body was found in a railway tunnel—approximate death between two and three weeks ago—and this Stuart Daws. I don't want this getting out just yet, mate. We've got evidence to believe that Daws killed the other victim."

"Really? So if he killed this bloke, then who killed him? More to the point, why? Any clues on that yet?"

"Haven't got the foggiest. I need a favour from you?" Hero asked.

"Go on. You know I'll always help if I can."

"A forensic sculptor has made up a clay face of our John Doe. I wondered if you would run the picture and a small story in the paper this evening?"

"I'll have a word with the boss, but I don't anticipate there being a problem with that, Hero. Can you fax the image over to me now?"

"I'll get on to it right away."

"What sort of thing do you want written in the article?"

"The usual for a murder enquiry. We need to keep certain things under wraps for now. Just the location, which I've already given you, and the TOD, which is approximately two to three weeks ago."

"Sure. Send the pic over, and while I'm waiting for it to arrive, I'll get the go-ahead from the boss. I can't see him not agreeing to run the story. Shall I put you down as the contact name for any possible leads with the punters?"

"Yes, I suppose you better. Cheers, mate."

Hero hung up and went over to the fax machine. He leaned against the windowsill, his arms folded, while he waited for the fax to send, contemplating the next plan of action. Without a formal identification, he couldn't do much. If only they could track down Foster and find a good reason to pull Cathy Daws in for questioning. Maybe his team's tenacity would strike lucky during the course of the day. *And maybe it won't!*

Hero left the station just after six that evening and made his way home to his wife and three children. Fay and the girls had left hospital on Saturday, and he and Fay had spent the weekend getting acquainted with the twins before Louie came home. He smiled at the thought of telling people he was the proud father of three kids. A couple of years ago, he would never have thought of himself as being father material. He was pleased he'd mended his ways and stopped turning to pints of beer at the pub for solace. He pulled into a petrol station to fill up his car, and when he went inside to pay, he stopped at the flower display near the doorway. He picked out the healthiest-looking bouquet. *They'll do. No one will be able to tell they were from a garage, will they?*

Arriving home, he called out, "Hi, sweetheart. I'm home." He was almost trampled as Louie came running into the hallway to see him. Hero succeeded in placing the bouquet on the bottom of the stairs before Louie jumped into his arms.

"Daddy, you're home."

He squeezed his son and kissed his cheek. "Hi, rascal. How was Grandma's?"

"Fun, but I missed you. Can we do something together this weekend, please?"

Hero placed his son back on the ground and picked up the flowers. "I don't see why not. Let me see what we can work out, all right?"

Louie ran back into the lounge. "Great."

Fay appeared in the lounge doorway. The black circles under her eyes told Hero that she'd had the day from hell. He presented the flowers and kissed her lovingly on the lips. "Bad day, hon?"

"Thank you for these. They're beautiful. Who would have thought I'd ever say that about flowers bought from a garage forecourt?" she teased then laughed gently when his face dropped.

"How the heck can you tell where I bought them? And by the way, they weren't cheap."

She kissed him again and turned to walk into the lounge. "Women just know about these things. Are you hungry?"

"You look done in, love. Let me finish the dinner off while you put your feet up."

"Janice was kind enough to drop by with a chicken casserole today. I'm just warming it through now. The girls have played me up today. They probably haven't got used to the different environment yet."

"I insist you sit down and I'll even do the clearing up, too, all right?"

She smiled and nodded in her son's direction. "You and Louie can do it together. He's already volunteered. It's nice to be surrounded by such caring men. I'm sure the girls and I will appreciate the help around the house in years to come."

He slammed the heel of his hand into his forehead. "Oh no, I walked right into that one, didn't I?"

"How was work?" Fay asked, following him through to the kitchen.

"The case is coming together nicely now. I suspect we'll still have a few twists and turns to overcome yet before we crack it, but at least it's progressing along the right lines now. That body we found the other day is now linked to the case we were already investigating."

"Good from your point of view. Not so good for the families and victims involved, though, eh?" Fay bent down to look at how dinner was fairing in the oven.

"Yeah, although I wouldn't afford them too much sympathy. We're hardly dealing with pillars of the community. They're a bunch of petty criminals, remember?"

"I know, but no one deserves for their lives to be ended so abruptly, no matter what crimes they've committed in the past."

"Yes, Oh Wise One. That smells delicious."

"Are you just saying that because I haven't made it?" she teased.

"Not at all. I wouldn't dream of being so rude. I'd never eat again if I did that. Anyway, it certainly smells better than the Vicks I've had to shove up my nose lately."

Fay's mouth twisted. "Eww… not sure I could slather that stuff up my nose on a daily basis."

He laughed. "It's hardly on a daily basis, but I understand where you're coming from. You seem to be taking over, as usual. Can I do anything to help?" Hero looked at the kitchen table and saw that it had already been laid. "Or has Louie beaten me to it?"

She leaned in and whispered, "You can check that he's placed the knives and forks the right way round for me. I left him to it and saw him changing them several times, bless him."

"At least he's trying to be helpful. He seems pleased to be back home with us."

"He is. He's brilliant with the girls. Sammy's great, too."

"Where is the cheeky mutt, anyway?"

"I put him in the garden just before you got home. Can you check he's all right?"

Hero pulled open the back door, and the Rottweiler was sitting in his usual Buddha position on the doorstep. His tail wagged when Hero crouched down to stroke him. "Been shut out, mate. Want some din-dins?"

The black-and-tan dog leapt to his feet and licked his lips. Hero held open the door for him to enter and prepared a dish of his favourite tinned meat and biscuits.

"Thanks, that's a great help," Fay said. She reached into the cupboard and pulled out three dinner plates. "Louie, can you wash your hands now? I'm dishing up."

"I'll just pop in and say hello to the girls." Hero started to walk out of the kitchen, but Fay stopped him.

"Leave it until after dinner. I've not long put them down for a nap. Don't give me that look. I know it's late for them to be catching forty winks, but they've been awake most of the day."

"It's all right. I promise not to tell your mother. You know that's a pet peeve of hers. She's the one who'd give you a hard time, love, not me."

"Thanks, I appreciate the support. Let's eat. I'm starving."

During the course of the meal, Louie kept them entertained with his chatterbox ways, and afterwards, Hero made Fay a herbal tea and ordered her to put her feet up while he and Louie washed up and tidied the kitchen. Despite feeling exhausted himself, Hero washed down all the surfaces thoroughly, conscious of the need to get rid of the pesky germs while the babies were at a vulnerable age. Then he went upstairs to check on his beautiful daughters. Zara was lying on her back, wide awake, when he leaned over the cot. He picked up his daughter and cradled her in his arms, grateful that she had come through the emergency operation without any problems. He kissed her cheek and swooned a little on the baby smells emanating from his small bundle of joy.

"It suits you." Fay's voice startled him.

"Fatherhood?"

"Yep." She came into the room, placed an arm around his back, and with her other hand, she pulled Zara's blanket away from her face. "I must say, I had my doubts if you'd take to this."

"*You* had doubts? I'm sure mine outweighed yours, love. I'm going to make sure you and the children never want for anything. I promise to support you every way possible from this day forward. You guys are my world."

Fay kissed him with tears welling up in her eyes. "We're so lucky to have you, Hero. I have no doubts that you'll do your utmost to care for us all in the future. Who knows what lies ahead of us? Zara was lucky to have come through her health scare, but I bet she'll turn out to be the strongest of the twins in the long run."

Hero placed his dozing daughter carefully back in the cot, and they left the infants' room together, arm in arm.

"I fancy pancakes for pudding. Do you think Louie will want some?"

Fay smiled in amusement. "I'm sure he'd love some. You should be resting, though. I'll make them for you."

"Oh no, I insist. You go and put your feet up."

Hero made the lemon and sugar pancakes then took them into the lounge, where they all tucked in. Hero flicked through the channels and stopped on Sky News when he saw the picture of his John Doe on the screen. He had a good feeling about the coverage and sensed that he would be busy at work the following morning, thanks to Dave's efforts and the local TV newsroom.

CHAPTER SEVEN

Hero decided to make his way into work early the next day. When the hands on the office wall clock hit eight o'clock, he was already in his office, attacking the morning post, trying to get ahead. He wanted the daily chore out of the way before he read through the list of messages the desk sergeant had handed him on the way in. He lasted all of ten minutes before the temptation took hold.

Julie knocked on the office door twenty minutes later. "Morning, sir. Any new leads from last night's coverage?"

"Come in and take a seat."

Julie sat opposite him. He studied her a little before returning to the messages. His partner seemed a little brighter that day, with a little more colour in her cheeks than she'd had the previous day. "How's your mum doing?"

"A bit better, thanks. The doctor has upped her pain-relief medication. It came with a warning that she didn't have long to live."

"Geez, I'm sorry, Julie. I meant what I said yesterday about taking time off. You only have to ask."

"I appreciate that. I'd rather be here than dwelling on the inevitable at home, sir." She held out her hand for her share of messages.

Hero nodded, understanding her need to get on with work to push the worry about her mother aside for the time being. He divided the pile and handed her half the messages.

"From what I can see so far, we've got three possible names."

"Let's hope we don't get many more to waste our time."

"My sentiments entirely." He jotted down the names on a piece of paper, leaving enough space for more information relating to each individual, which he hoped to add later that morning.

When the rest of the team arrived, Hero and Julie joined them in the incident room. "Listen up, peeps. Our number-one priority today is to find out who our latest victim is. Julie and I have been going through the call messages from last night's airing and found three potential names. There might be more, but I've gone for the names that more than one caller has put to the victim. Let's get cracking on this. I'd like a result by ten o'clock. All right?"

The sound of scraping chairs and computers being booted up filled the room. Hero bought a cup of coffee from the vending machine then tackled his own mundane chore of answering his mail.

Within half an hour, several cheers broke out in the incident room, and Hero ran through to find out what all the commotion was about. "Well? Don't keep me in suspenders?"

"Over here, sir." Foxy raised an arm.

His stomach churned as he looked at the man's image. "My God, that has to be him, doesn't it? Mark Lomax, do we have a last known address for him, Foxy?"

"Just getting that for you now, sir. I'll print off his criminal record, too."

"Another petty, I take it?"

"Looks that way to begin with." She pointed at the screen. "He seems to have moved up the ladder in the last few months. He's wanted in connection with an armed robbery of a jewellers' in the city."

"Interesting. Chase the crime number up for me, will you?"

"Will do. Let me find you his address first. Here we go. Ten Millbank Street, Salford."

"Well, that puts him within spitting distance of the Daws's, doesn't it? I can foresee another visit to the compassionate Cathy Daws coming up in my not-too-distant future. Julie, are you okay to come out with me today?"

"Yes, sir. Now?"

"Why not." Hero fetched his jacket from the office before he and Julie left for Lomax's address.

Most of the houses on Millbank Street had boarded-up windows at the front, and the whole area was in dire need of either bulldozing or regeneration. Hero had no idea which would benefit it the best.

"Here it is, sir." Julie pointed out the house.

Hero searched the street for a safe place to park, where he could keep a close eye on the vehicle from the house. "Let's see what we can find out, shall we?"

The two detectives got out of the car. Hero knocked on the red front door and stood back. Julie did the same on the other side of the opening. The walls of the house shielded them, just in case someone inside the house tried to shoot at them through the front door.

They waited another minute or two before Hero knocked a second time. There was still no answer, so Hero suggested they should each knock on the neighbour's door to either side. Hero tried the door to the right.

Eventually, an old man dressed in soiled clothing opened the door to Hero. "Yeah, what d'ya want?"

Hero showed his ID. "I'm looking for Mark Lomax. Does he live here?"

"Yep, ain't seen him for weeks. What's the little shit done now?"

"Actually, I was checking to see if he shared his house with anyone? Any idea about that?"

"Nope. He's a loner, that one. You didn't answer me. What's he done?"

"His body was found a few days ago. I'm here to inform any relatives he might have of his death. I don't suppose you have a contact address for any possible friends or relatives, do you?"

The man looked him up and down as if Hero were mad. "What am I, sonny? His bloody keeper?"

"I'm sorry. It's important that we find his next of kin so that they can make the appropriate arrangements for his funeral."

"I understand that. I'm sorry, but I keep myself to myself, don't I? I don't mix with the buggers around here."

"What about his mates? Did he have regular visits from friends?"

"You're not hearing me, sonny. Do you think I've got nothing better to do all day than sit staring out my window, spying on my neighbours? What do you take me for?"

Hero dug in his pocket and pulled out a business card. "Ring me if you think of anything once I'm gone, please?" He turned his back and took two steps towards his partner before he heard the man clear his throat.

"There was a couple of people."

Hero returned to lean against the wall of the man's house. "A couple, as in a man and a woman?"

"Yep. Nothing fancy. Well, you wouldn't expect that around these parts anyway, I suppose."

"How regular? The visits, I mean. Did they come and see Lomax often?" Hero asked, raising his voice as his excitement grew.

"I got your meaning the first time, sonny. I ain't stupid—or deaf, for that matter."

"Sorry. The visitors?" Hero queried a second time, cursing himself for not bringing a photo of either Cathy or Stuart Daws with him.

"Regular enough. Maybe once every few weeks." He pointed at his furrowed forehead as he thought. "Hang on a minute. There's another man who comes to see him, too. Older than the man and woman, but just as rough-looking."

"If I came back with some photo IDs, would you be able to pick these three out?"

"I don't know. Me eyesight ain't what it used to be."

"But it's worth a try, eh?"

"Yep, all right. I'll do what I can, but you've gotta come to me. I ain't going down the nick. I don't tend to leave the house much. You don't know what mess you might come home to. Kids round here are a pain in the arse, loads of gangs. You could always return mob handed and help us rid the area of these little tykes. You know, one good turn deserves another, don't it?"

"I'll see what I can do regarding uniformed police keeping an eye on the area while my team try and rid the city of all the murderers walking the streets. How's that?"

"All right, sonny. No need to get your y-fronts all in a twist now. I was just making a point and asking for some assistance. Nowt wrong in that, is there?"

"Sorry, okay. I'll send a member of my team over this afternoon. Is that okay?"

"And what about your guys keeping the streets safe. You gonna sort that out, too?"

Hero sighed; the man had him by the short and curlies, and he knew it. "I'll see what I can do. I can't be any fairer than that, can I?"

"All right, that'll do for me. Don't go sending your mate around here until I've had lunch. I don't appreciate anyone disturbing me while I'm eating, right?"

"Okay, what if we say two o'clock? Does that suit you?" Hero found it difficult to suppress his smile.

"Yep, that'll do." The man slammed the door shut in Hero's face.

"Nice character." Hero snorted as he and Julie returned to the car.

"It takes all sorts, as my old gran used to say. Who are you thinking of sending back here this afternoon?"

"I thought I'd give Jason the privilege. Do you think I should send Lance, too?"

"I think it would be better to send two rather than one. That way, one man could keep an eye on the car while the other goes in to see the old man."

"Damn, I never got the man's name. Never mind, we've got his address."

Back at the station, Hero gave Jason the man's address and told him to gather the relevant photos and go to the man's home after lunch.

Then Hero moved on to see if Foxy had any news for him. "Anything on the bank job yet?"

"I've got the crime number, and it would appear that there were two people involved in the actual robbery and one waiting in the car outside."

"Any camera footage of the men involved? I take it the other robber was male?"

"Yes, sir, on both counts, although the image is very grainy. Both robbers wore ski masks, but Lomax saw fit to tear his mask off towards the end of the robbery."

"How strange. Would it be too simple to say he removed the mask because he felt suffocated wearing it? What if that's what got him killed? Hmm… you know what? The more I think about it, the more I'm inclined to believe this is the motive the killer needed to attack or punish him, for his stupidity."

Foxy nodded. "It's certainly plausible, sir. If Daws was the other robber, that is."

Hero glanced at his watch. "Okay, I'm going out again. There's someone else we know who could shed some light on this. I might just catch her at home before her shift starts at the pub. Julie, are you ready to go out again?"

He looked over in time to see his partner's eyes roll upwards. She placed both hands on the desk and levered herself to her feet once more. "Yes, sir," she replied, tedium evident in her tone. She snatched her jacket off the back of the chair and walked towards him.

"Just think of the exercise we'll be getting going up and down all those stairs. You'll think back and thank me for this one day, Julie, when you have a saggy bottom." His attempt at humour only added sourness to her already-foul mood.

Julie grunted as she pushed past him, through the door to the incident room without holding it open for him to join her. Hero looked down at Foxy and cringed. "Oops, did I say something wrong?"

Foxy chuckled. "First rule in the *One hundred ways not to piss off a woman handbook*, sir, is never to discuss a woman's weight or saggy bits!"

Hero laughed and set off after his fuming partner with Foxy's warning imprinted in his mind.

CHAPTER EIGHT

The scowl on Cathy's face when she opened the door to the two detectives prepared Hero for an unwelcome and uncomfortable visit. Swiftly taking control of the situation, he barged past her and into the hallway before she had the chance to shut the door in their faces. "Mind if we come in? Thanks."

Cathy's scowl intensified. "Do I have a choice?" she spat at them.

"No. We'll talk in here, shall we?" He stormed into the lounge with the noise of the front door slamming ringing in his ears.

Cathy marched into the room after Hero and Julie. She threw herself on the sofa and crossed her arms in defiance. "What do you want? Can't a woman grieve in peace?"

"Come now, Cathy, if you were that cut up about your husband's death, you wouldn't be back at work so soon, would you?"

"A lot you know then. How the fuck do you think I'm supposed to manage without bringing some money in? I don't get widow benefits like they hand out to privileged bastards like you. If I don't turn up for work, that's it. No money, end of!"

"Less of the attitude, Cathy. I appreciate everyone isn't as 'privileged' as you call it, like us, but surely your boss wouldn't have been that *heartless* not to have allowed you a day off right after finding out about your husband's death?"

"Like I've already said, you know nothin'. Why are you here? I told you all I know the other day. Unless you take pleasure in hounding grieving widows, do ya'?"

"We're not here to hound you, Mrs. Daws. We simply want to ask you a few more questions in light of new evidence that has come to our attention."

She narrowed one eye. "What new evidence?"

Hero got the impression she was playacting. She had more than an inkling about what he was hinting at; he was almost positive about that. "Mind if I sit down? It's been a hectic morning. A cup of coffee would go down a treat, too. I don't suppose there's any chance of getting one though, is there?"

She muttered two words that shot his hint down in flames. "Tight budget."

"Okay, it was worth a try. Right, what if I throw a couple of names your way? The game is I tell you a name, and you say whether you have any kind of relationship with these people or not. Got that?"

"What names? What kind of relationships are you on about?"

He offered up a fake smile. "Let's start with Stan Foster. Do you know him?"

Her gaze dropped to the floor. "What about him?"

"So, you're not denying you know the man?" Hero pressed.

"Why should I? He is... was my husband's friend."

"That's what we thought. I seem to recall the landlord of the New Inn telling us that Foster and your husband were seen drinking together at the bar on the night he was murdered."

"Yeah, what of it? You forgot to mention they were getting pissed on my money... he was always a leech like that."

Hero nodded his understanding of her angry comment. "Any idea where Stan might be now?"

"No. Should I have?"

Hero bit the inside of his mouth before he asked his next question. "We've been to his flat to try and get a statement from him, but he appears to have vanished. Is there somewhere else he stays? Does he have a girlfriend, perhaps?"

"How should I friggin' know? I barely know the man."

"Really? Okay, here's another name for you to consider." He paused and waited for her eyes to connect with his.

Eventually, she looked up at him.

"Mark Lomax. Do you know him?"

Her eyes immediately dropped again, proving that she did know him, if only by name.

"Sort of. Why?" she mumbled, burying her chin deep into her chest.

"It's been discovered that your husband was friends with him, and that they carried out an armed robbery together. According to our records, they hit a jewellers' in Manchester city centre a few months back. Did you or do you know about that?"

She shook her head. "Nope, don't know a thing."

"Mrs. Daws, look at me."

The woman's head slowly rose.

"I think you're lying."

"Think what you like. You can't prove that I'm involved in this," she challenged, holding his stare.

Hero nodded. "You're right. We can't—yet. However, you have my word that I won't stop digging until I can implicate you in both crimes. Oops, I mean all three crimes."

"What *three* crimes? All you've mentioned is Stuart's death and some kind of hold up. What's this third crime you're on about?" She seemed genuinely confused.

He said his next sentence slowly, ensuring she got the full impact of his words. "One, your husband's *murder*, not death."

Mrs. Daws's eyes almost popped out of her head.

"The robbery, which we believe your husband was deeply involved in and…" He paused as she sat forward in her chair. "And the final part of the equation is the murder of Mark Lomax."

Cathy jumped to her feet and ran at him, her arms flailing, not in the least bit bothered where she struck him. Julie caught one of the woman's wrists, but before she could grip the other one, Cathy's fist connected with Julie's eye.

"You, bitch, I'll get you for assaulting a police officer."

Hero helped his partner try to calm the woman down. He withdrew his cuffs and slapped them on Cathy, who was out of control and screaming all sorts of obscenities at them. He read the woman her rights then put her in the back of the car. Julie climbed in the rear of the vehicle beside the demented woman.

That went well! Not exactly the reaction I was expecting.

Sensing what deep shit she was in, Cathy Daws calmed down a few minutes into the journey. Neither Hero nor Julie spoke to the woman until they reached the station.

Julie hauled the woman by the cuffs across the backseat of the car. "Get out."

Hero locked the car, and with the detectives either side of the suspect, the three of them walked into the station. "I'll handle this. You go and get cleaned up," Hero told Julie.

"Are you going to interview her right away or let her stew in the cell for now?" Julie asked over her shoulder as she walked away.

"We'll have to wait for her solicitor to arrive before we can question her, so she'll stew for a while first," Hero replied over the suspect's head.

"What have we got here then, Inspector?" the desk sergeant asked, his pen poised to fill out the arrest form.

"Cathy Daws… I want her arrested for assaulting a police officer. More serious charges, along the lines of attempted murder or even murder will likely follow after we've questioned her."

"What? I haven't done anything. They provoked me into attacking them, forced their way into my house, and then started insinuating that I've killed people. I haven't, I swear. Christ. I'm the victim here. My bloody husband was found murdered a few days ago, remember? I want a solicitor. I'm not dealing with this crap alone. I've heard what happens in these places when things aren't going *your* way. Some of my mates have been beaten up by your lot trying to make them talk. Well, it won't happen to me. I know my rights."

"You do indeed, Daws. That's why I've instructed a solicitor to join us. Unless you can afford one of your own, which is highly improbable, considering the amount of pleading poverty we've heard today."

"Just get me a solicitor, preferably not a bent one. I know what you lot get up to, remember?" she added a second time, to emphasise her point.

The desk sergeant motioned for a female police constable to join them. The PC went through the procedure of frisking Cathy and looking for anything she could try to hang herself with, but found nothing. After the custody form was complete and Daws had signed it, the sergeant said, "Take this nice young lady to the cells, will you, Nixon?"

The PC guided Cathy Daws toward the cells. Hero watched her walk away, all her venom and fight subsided, for the moment. "Thanks. Ring me when the solicitor arrives, and I'll come straight down to question her. Can you also keep an interview room free?"

The desk sergeant laughed. "That shouldn't be too difficult, sir. It's reasonably quiet around here today, for a change."

In the distance, the metal cell door banged. The constable returned and handed Hero his cuffs. In need of a coffee fix, he made his way upstairs. It had been a long day already, and it was only half over.

Hero ended up kicking his heels in his office for the next thirty minutes, until finally, the call he'd been waiting for came through. "DI Nelson."

"The solicitor has arrived, sir," the desk sergeant informed him.

"I'll be down in a jiffy."

Hero marched into the incident room and approached Julie. "Ouch, that looks nasty. I'm about to question Daws. Do you want to join me, or would you give it a miss? I'm happy either way."

"You can definitely count me in on this one. I want the bitch to feel guilty for what she's done to me." Julie touched the plaster above her discoloured eye.

Hero doubted very much if Daws would ever feel guilty for lashing out at a copper. Julie was kidding herself if she thought that about the woman. Hero suspected that Daws was more likely to take pleasure in seeing the damage she'd done to his partner, and he even predicted a few sniggers at Julie's expense.

"Right, let's see what we can get out of her then. Maybe she'll surprise us and open up more, considering her surroundings."

"I doubt that, sir." Julie trotted alongside him, through the corridor and down the stairs.

The assigned solicitor turned out to be a long-standing acquaintance of Hero's. He and James Boulten had been at the same school together in their teens. They nodded a greeting rather than letting on to the suspect that they were friends, given the way Daws had already bandied about unsubstantiated accusations of bent coppers and unscrupulous solicitors.

Before initiating the interview, Julie said the necessary announcement for the tape: the date, time and the names of the occupants in the room.

"Mrs. Daws, can you tell us why you felt the need to attack my partner, DS Shaw, earlier today?"

Cathy stayed silent, eyes cast down at her clenched hands on the table.

Hero shrugged at the solicitor, hoping he would prompt his client to answer, but he didn't. He tried again to provoke a response. "Okay, fair enough. That's one charge you'll definitely be charged with at the end of this interview." He turned to his partner and winked. "Maybe the suspect will do the right thing and issue you an apology afterwards, DS Shaw."

"No, I won't," Daws hissed.

Julie shook her head at Hero. "People have been banged up for less, sir."

"All right, I'm going to cut in here," Boulten said. "Less of the crap, detectives, and get on with questioning my client. Neither of us want to be in this room longer than necessary, do we?"

"Granted. Perhaps you better instruct your client that it would be in her best interest to answer my questions promptly in that case, Mr. Boulten?"

"When the need arises, I won't hesitate to do that, Inspector. I assure you. Carry on."

Hero smiled tightly. "Mrs. Daws, can you tell us what your relationship is with Stan Foster?"

Daws looked at her brief, who nodded for her to respond. "I've told you already," she muttered.

"For the tape, Mrs. Daws, nice and clearly, if you don't mind?"

"He's a mate of my husband, or he was. Like I told you back at my house, I don't really know the man, other than to say hello to in the street."

"Are you telling me the man has never been in your house before?"

"Briefly, on a couple of occasions."

"So, am I to gather from that you don't have a deep friendship with this man?" Hero asked.

"Deep friendship? What the friggin' hell is that supposed to mean? The guy turns my stomach." Her nose wrinkled in disgust.

"It was a simple question. Maybe I didn't make myself clear. I wondered if you knew the man or other members of his family? What else did you think I meant?" Hero asked. Her attempts to put him off the scent aroused his suspicions. Her body language wasn't a true reflection of what was coming out of her mouth.

"I told you, I barely know him. I'm not sure what you want me to tell you." Her wicked grin bared uneven yellowing teeth that made Hero's stomach churn. "I can make up some lies if it'll help. Is that what you want? Me to pretend I know this man more than I actually do? My mates have always said that you guys like to put words into people's mouths. Is that what you're trying to do?"

"Not at all. Just speak the truth, and hopefully, we'll be able to verify what you say. If, however, you choose to lead us up the wrong route with your answers, then we'll make sure the Crown Prosecution Service throw the book at you. It's your choice."

Cathy's face hardened into a deep scowl reminiscent of the one she'd given him at her house earlier. "I've already told you the truth. How many more times do I have to say it? Yes, he's been in my house, but I'm always far too busy running around after my husband to sit and chat with his friends. Well, that's what I used to do, before..."

Boulten raised his hand. "Please refrain from upsetting my client, Inspector. It is my understanding that people going through the grieving process should be handled with compassion and understanding. Am I making myself clear?"

"Perfectly clear, Mr. Boulten, although I'm at a loss to know what I've said or done to step out of line on that front."

"Just a word of warning, Inspector. You'd be wise to carry on questioning my client with caution and a smattering of empathy."

Hero gave a brief nod. "Very well." With his gaze fixed on the solicitor, he asked, "Mrs. Daws, can you tell me what you know about an armed robbery that was carried out at Curtiss Nash's, the jewellers' in Manchester city centre, a few months ago?"

"Nothing. Again, I told you that earlier at my house, but did you believe me? No, you didn't. Instead, you manhandled me, shoved me in the back of your car, and dragged me in here for questioning."

"That was hardly the case, and you know it. We pulled you in because you assaulted DS Shaw. Oh, and me, for that matter, but I'm willing to let that charge slip. I think you have enough possible crimes on your plate for now. Of course, we could always revisit the assault charge in the future if necessary. So, just to clarify, you're saying that your husband told you absolutely nothing about the robbery?" Hero asked.

"Already answered by my client, Inspector. Move on, if you will? Not that I can see any connection yet. Maybe you care to enlighten me as to why you've jumped from asking my client about this Foster man to her husband's involvement in a robbery?"

"My mistake, Mr. Boulten. I should have made you aware from the start that your client is being questioned about three different crimes that have been highlighted since we started investigating the death of her husband. We're simply trying to piece everything together. I find it hard to believe that your client knows very little or nothing, as she has already stated, about the events. So, I'm going to repeat my question, if I may? What did your husband tell you about his involvement in the robbery?"

"Absolutely nothing, I'm telling you. Why the heck don't you believe me?"

"At the moment, Cathy, it's very hard to believe a word that comes out of your mouth. Let's see if we can change that, yes?"

Cathy Daws turned to her solicitor. "I don't know anything. Please make him understand that. Come on, do your job. That's what I'm paying you for, isn't it?"

Mr. Boulten shuffled uncomfortably in his seat. "Actually, you're not paying me. Legal aid are. Maybe it would be best to tell the inspector what you know from the outset."

Cathy snorted and snarled at him, "You're all tarred with the same brush." She slumped back in her chair. "You might as well arrest me now and be done with it because nothing I say is going to change your mind, is it?"

"If you're innocent in all three crimes, then fair enough. However, you really need to start being open with us. That's the idea of this interview, for you to help us with our enquiries whilst eliminating yourself as a suspect. You have to admit that one crime being attributed to one person can be deemed as unfortunate, but three crimes coming to light in one week involving one family is more than a little suspicious."

"I suppose so. I'm in the dark about this. You have to believe me. You said my husband was murdered and that you suspected I did it. I'm confused about that because I've given you a perfectly good alibi for the time of his death. But you seem keen to ignore it."

"Is that right, Inspector?" Boulten asked, looking up from his notebook and tapping his pen thoughtfully against his square, stubble-free chin.

"Well, yes. But it doesn't mean to say that Mrs. Daws can't be implicated in another way," Hero pointed out.

"Meaning?" both Cathy and Boulten asked in unison.

"*Meaning* that Mrs. Daws might have paid someone to do the deed for her."

"Piss off!" Cathy shouted. She nudged her solicitor with her elbow and demanded, "Can he say that? Accuse me like that without proof?"

"No, he can't." His brow furrowed, and he said to Hero, "You can't fling accusations like that around the room, Inspector, without at least some foundation of the truth being attached."

"It wasn't an accusation, Mr. Boulten. I was merely laying all the facts on the table. Three crimes in one week, and all the clues are leading back to your client's door. It's hard to argue against the facts. I'm sure you'll agree on that count, yes?"

Grudgingly, the solicitor had to agree. "I suppose so, when you put it like that. But if my client states over and over again that she knows nothing about either of the crimes, where does that leave us, Inspector?" Boulten glanced at his wristwatch.

"Sorry, are we keeping you, Mr. Boulten?" Hero tried hard to keep the amusement from tinting in his voice when he realised that it must be fast approaching the brief's lunchtime.

"Well, I do have a luncheon appointment that I should keep. If you can wrap this up early, I'd appreciate…"

Hero shook his head. "Sorry, no can do. We're here for the duration, I'm afraid. I can get the sergeant to nip out for sandwiches, but we have no intention of letting your client go before we've thoroughly questioned her and received satisfactory answers to my questions. Do you need to make a call, Mr. Boulten?"

The solicitor stood up. "I'll be back in a moment."

"Mr. Boulten is leaving the room," Julie said then turned off the tape.

Hero seized the opportunity to talk to Daws during her solicitor's absence. "Cathy, come on. The sooner you open up, the quicker we can all get out of here. Are you with me on that?"

Exasperated, Cathy threw her arms out to the side and sighed heavily. "I'm tired, desperate for a fag, and hungry, and for the umpteenth time, I know fuck all about what Stuart was up to. If he did rob the jewellers, I'm bloody livid that I never saw any of the dosh from it, if you must know. But then I'm not surprised. His money has always been his money. Without me working and paying for all the bills, we would have been kicked out of our home years ago. And that's the truth. This is all news to me. I swear."

The solicitor came back into the room at that point, and Cathy shut up. "Have I missed something? You know the rules about questioning a client in my absence, Inspector?"

"I didn't. Cathy and I were just having a chat. There's no law against that, is there? Get your lunch date cancelled in time, did you?" Hero stretched his mouth into a large grin.

"No and yes, in that order, to answer both your questions. Now, where were we?" Boulten settled into his seat, and Julie restarted the recorder.

"We were just asking Mrs. Daws what she knew about the burglary her husband, Stuart, was involved in. So you're telling me that in the last few months, your husband's spending habits haven't altered at all?"

"Not that I've noticed, apart from the night he was murdered, and we know why that was. He robbed my housekeeping money and pissed it up the wall with Foster," she stated, crossing her arms.

"Ah yes, and nothing else you can think of over the past few weeks or months? Has he visited the pub more often than usual perhaps?"

"He'd have a job. He goes down the pub every day. Did," she corrected, not for the first time during the interview.

"Maybe he's had more visitors coming to the house lately, more than usual?"

She shook her head. "Nope."

After getting nowhere for several hours, Hero moved on to the third and final crime Mr. Daws had links to. Hero thought Cathy was sure to know about it, despite her reluctance to admit it.

"Okay, we'll leave that for now and move on to the murder of Mark Lomax." He paused to see what kind of reaction he received from her after the way she'd charged at him back at her house. This time, however, the woman remained in her seat and twiddled her thumbs. "So, what can you tell me about Mark Lomax?"

"Nothing."

"That's not the impression I got earlier. When I mentioned Lomax's name back at your house, you ran at me. Why?"

Cathy's gaze remained on the table, and she slowly shook her head.

"What is it, Mrs. Daws? What aren't you telling us?"

"I know nothing. I just can't believe you're trying to pin this crap on me. Why won't you believe me?"

"I'm trying to. Honestly, I am. If you open up and tell us what you know, then it could make the difference in so many ways."

"Such as?" She glanced at her solicitor for guidance. He nodded, indicating that he thought she should speak the truth if she knew anything.

"I've already stated that I would put in a good word with the prosecution service. Maybe we could look at sending you to an open prison once you've been convicted. That's the best I can do."

"Why? Why do I have to go to prison? All I've done, all that I'm going to ever admit to, is that I hit your partner. That, I swear to God, is the only crime I've committed, ever."

"If that's the case, then why did you overreact when I mentioned Lomax's name?"

She heaved a heavy sigh. "How would you react if someone asked you about the *murder* of someone? I've already said how some people I know have been fixed up by you lot. Now the same bloody thing is happening to me, ain't it? How the hell would you react to such a question? Tell me that?" Her eyes bored into Hero's in a defiant challenge.

"My client does appear to have a good point there, Inspector, doesn't she? Considering what stress she's been under in the past few days due to the loss of her husband, it wouldn't be unreasonable to forgive her for such an outburst, would it?" Mr. Boulten said, sporting what appeared to be a triumphant grin.

"I'm willing to admit that her reaction would be justifiable had I hounded her on the point, but that wasn't the case, Mr. Boulten. Was it, Mrs. Daws?"

"No. I just heard the word *murder* and flipped. I'm sorry for that. Sorry that you're willing to hold it against me."

Hero watched the woman's eyes mist up. Not moved in the slightest, he put her pretence at being upset down to her playing a part again. "Providing you haven't done anything wrong, there was no need for you to react that way. Now, tell the truth. Did you know Mark Lomax?"

"This is the truth, no!" Daws said adamantly.

"So your husband has never uttered his name?"

"No. Not that I can remember. Not that our relationship is what you would call chatty. I went to work, and he spent most of his time down the pub, a different pub to where I work. If we were that close, he'd want to drink where I worked, wouldn't he?"

Hero thought over her point and nodded. "Well, let me tell you what we know then." He looked down at his notes then back up at the suspect. "Mark Lomax's body was found in a tunnel at the end of last week. The estimated time of death is approximately two to three weeks ago."

The corners of Cathy's mouth turned down, and she shrugged. "So?"

Hero picked up his pen and pointed at her with it. "Here's the interesting part, Cathy. We've run extensive DNA tests on the victim's corpse, which by the way, was in a pretty gruesome state after stray dogs had munched on it, and the tests came back positive for your husband's DNA. How do you suppose that happened, Cathy?"

She sat upright in her chair and looked at her solicitor then back at Hero. "How the fuck should I know?"

"Just a minute. There's more to add to this little conundrum."

"More?" Her fringe moved as her forehead creased into a frown.

"Yes, we have reason to believe that Mark Lomax was an accomplice of your husband's on the jewellery burglary he carried out. And you still maintain you don't know the man?"

"Yes, I mean, *no*, I don't know him." She buried her head in her hands. "You have to believe me. Why did Stu have to get involved in all of this shit? Why?"

"That's what we're going to find out, Mrs. Daws, either with your help or without it."

"I would tell you if I knew anything, if only to get you off my back and me out of here. You have to believe me," she pleaded yet again.

Boulten placed his notebook on the desk. "I think we'll leave it there now, Inspector. All we seem to be doing is chasing round and round like a demented dog after his tail. It's obvious to me that my client knows nothing about either of the crimes you've mentioned. Therefore, I'm insisting that you let her go, without charge."

"Without charge? I'm not sure we can agree to that, Mr. Boulten. We have the assault of a police officer to throw at your client before the day is out. One last chance, Mrs. Daws. What do you know about either crime?"

The woman squared her shoulders. "My final word is that I know nothing. And I'm sorry about your partner's black eye."

Defeated, although reluctant to show it, Hero faced his partner. "Would you like to go ahead with your complaint, DS Shaw?"

"I think due to the stress Mrs. Daws was under, I'm willing to withdraw the complaint, sir."

Hero only just managed to prevent his mouth from falling open in shock. Julie's willingness to drop the charges had come out of the blue and floored him. Mrs. Daws let out a relieved breath, and Hero sharply turned to look at her. "That's very magnanimous of DS Shaw, wouldn't you agree, Mrs. Daws?"

"Yes. Thank you. I'm sorry."

"I pronounce this interview terminated. If you think of anything at all in the coming days that will help us piece the puzzle together, Mrs. Daws, will you contact us right away?" Hero handed her a business card.

"I will."

Julie turned off the tape while Hero saw Mrs. Daws and Mr. Boulten out. They stopped at the front desk to gather the woman's personal effects before exiting the main door of the building.

Walking up the stairs to the incident room, Julie caught up with Hero. "What do you think?"

"About Daws? I'm not sure. I hate to admit it, but I think she's telling the truth, at least with some of it. Don't ask me which parts. It's just an instinct."

Hero nodded, although he held back his reservations. "Let's put her to one side for now and see where the rest of the evidence trail leads us. Jason and Lance should be back by now from questioning the old man. Maybe they'll have something of relevance to share."

CHAPTER NINE

As it turned out, Jason was looking mighty pleased with himself when Hero and Julie joined the rest of the team in the incident room.

"Looks promising. What did the old gent have to say, Jason?" Hero perched on the desk closest to Jason's.

"I took him photos of both Cathy and Stuart Daws—"

"Hold back on the enthusiasm just a second, Jason. How did you get a picture of the wife, Cathy Daws? She doesn't have a record, does she?"

"Nope." Jason smiled awkwardly. "I kind of used my initiative, sir."

"How exactly?"

"When Daws came in earlier, her arrival was on the station's security camera. I asked the desk sergeant if I could take a still photo from the footage."

"Clever. Some might call you a smartarse, but not I. Carry on?" Hero nodded approvingly at the youngster.

Jason beamed with appreciation. "Anyway, I'm not sure what Mrs. Daws said during her interview, sir—"

"She told Julie and me that she didn't know Lomax. Go on. You're going to tell me that she's taken us for fools, aren't you?" Hero said.

"Well… I personally wouldn't put it that way myself, sir. However, according to Mr. Wilson—that's the man's name—she has visited Lomax's house on several occasions, with the other deceased victim, Stuart Daws."

Hero stood up and paced the area, running an angry hand through his short hair. "What the…? How in God's name did I let her trick me like that? Right, from now on, we hit that woman with everything we've got. I couldn't give a toss if she's grieving or not. Perhaps she killed her husband, too."

"But, she has a trusted alibi, sir," Julie pointed out from where she was seated at her desk.

"So she says. Maybe she took a break around the time her husband was killed," Hero said, walking over to the noticeboard to look at the clues and suspects he'd written down.

Jason joined him at the board. "Are you thinking that Foster picked her up, and they carried out the crime together?"

"I am. Let's see how far the locations are. Work out the timings, the probabilities of her involvement, despite her saying she was on duty that night?"

Jason rushed back to his desk. "On it, sir."

Hero was still running through the main players and clues when Jason returned a few minutes later. "I'd say we have an approximate time of thirty minutes for Cathy to get from one location to another. That's not taking into consideration how long the actual crime took to commit."

Hero tutted and leaned his shoulder against the wall. "It's not long enough, is it? Her boss would have noticed her missing during that time, surely?"

"I think so, sir. Frustrating though that is."

"But the person getting out of that vehicle did appear to be female, yes? Let's have another look at the footage just to make sure. It could have been a short man, I suppose, thinking about it."

They evaluated the footage again and came to the same conclusion that the movements likely belonged to a woman rather than a man. The question was how could he tie Cathy Daws to her husband's murder? Hero clicked his fingers. "Apart from getting a warrant to search Cathy's house, which we can't obtain without just cause, the only thing left open to us is to do a thorough search of the area. Yes, I know SOCO will be doing that close to the scene." Hero tapped the image on the monitor. "But we need to be searching in this area here. It's a long shot, but maybe, just maybe, the murderer dropped something as they got out of the vehicle. Jason? Do you fancy going to the scene for a couple of hours? Take Lance with you, eh?"

Lance groaned when Hero mentioned his name. Without turning around to face him, Hero called out, "Something wrong, Powell?"

After clearing his throat Lance shouted back, "No, sir. Everything is tickety boo with me."

"Good, glad to hear it." Hero clapped his hands, urging his team to get a move on. "Julie, fancy a ride out to Foster's flat?"

"But he's on the missing list, sir. I doubt that he's likely to turn up there, knowing we're after him."

"Well, let's go round there anyway. I want to see what the neighbours have to say about things. Jason's already come up trumps with Lomax's neighbour. Perhaps we can slot another piece into the puzzle with Foster's neighbours. Come on. While I'm explaining it to you, we could be out there. We're wasting time around here."

Julie followed him downstairs and out to the car, dragging her feet a little. Hero chose to ignore her obvious sulking and drummed his fingers on the steering wheel until she jumped in the passenger seat. Their journey to Foster's flat was silent.

When they reached their destination, Hero turned to Julie. "Let's have it. What's your problem with the task, Julie?"

"I just think it'll turn out to be a waste of time, and we could be doing something useful instead." Julie stared straight ahead at the row of shops below the flat they had come to visit.

"Such as? You tell me where and what else we could be doing right now, and I'll happily change direction on this case. I suspect Foster called me, remember? That reeks of a guilty conscience when suspects do that. You know how these things go, right?"

Julie fidgeted in her seat and thought over what he'd said. Eventually, she looked his way, a frown wrinkling her forehead. "All right, maybe there isn't anything else to go on right at this minute…"

"Precisely, Sergeant. Since when am I in the habit of wasting my time? If there were any other leads to go with right now, I'd be following them up in a shot, agreed?"

"Yes, sir. Sorry to doubt your decisions. Can we get in there now?" Julie opened the door and got out of the car before Hero could respond.

He was willing to accept she had other, more important things on her plate and was prepared to give her some slack because of the personal burden she was lugging around with her, but not for much longer. Granted, his partner rarely did cartwheels of joy when she worked alongside him, but depending on how the next few hours panned out and if Julie's attitude didn't improve, he would be forced to consider her position, at least until her personal life changed.

Hero locked the car and looked up at the flat. "I should have checked before. Have you got copies of the photos of the Daws?"

Julie searched her large handbag, pulled out a file, and nodded as she handed it to him. "Of course."

"Great stuff. Let's split up when we get up there, okay? We'll try Foster's flat first, though."

The stairwell was full of the usual graffiti, attacking the police and the government, found in rundown estates. Hero was thankful there weren't any signs of the typical smells and other disgusting traces of human bodily functions that they normally stumbled across.

Hero knocked on the door to the flat. After receiving no reply, he crouched and looked through the letterbox to determine if there was movement inside. "Mr. Foster, it's the police," he shouted. "If you're in there, open up."

The security chain on the next-door neighbour's front door banged against the wood. The door creaked open, and a little old lady's voice called out, "He's not there."

Hero straightened up and walked over to the woman's door. He flashed his warrant card and smiled. "When was the last time you saw him, Mrs...?"

"Taylor." Seeming more secure with the knowledge that she was dealing with the police, the woman opened the door a bit wider.

"Do you mind if we come in for a quick chat, Mrs. Taylor?"

"Well, the place is in a mess. The home help woman hasn't turned up again. That's the second time in as many weeks. They all need to be given the boot. Most of them are bloody foreigners who speak crappy English when they're here. I used to love it when Maud was my appointed home help. We'd have a natter for hours, while she carried out her duties, of course. Sorry, I'm rambling. Come in."

Hero and Julie followed the woman through to a small lounge cluttered with old furniture. Lying on one of the old tapestry-covered chairs was a cat curled up into a tight ball. "Shoo, Charlie. Let the nice man sit down."

"Don't bother on my count. I spend most of my time sitting behind a desk anyway. It'll do me good to stand for a while."

The cat woke, gave Hero a sleepy, cursory glance, and promptly fell asleep again. Julie stood beside Hero, also turning down the seat the old woman offered. Mrs. Taylor eased her heavy frame into the sofa beside the gas fire, which was throwing out just enough heat to take the chill off the room.

"Getting back to Mr. Foster, when was the last time you saw him?" Hero asked, nodding at Julie and gesturing for her to take notes.

"It's hard to say. Maybe a week ago. I've heard him in the flat since then, of course, but haven't laid eyes on him as such."

"In that case, can you tell us when was the last time you heard him in the flat?"

"It has to be a few days now, maybe the weekend. I haven't really thought about it, not until now. What's the problem? Is he in some kind of trouble?"

"Maybe. At this point, his name has cropped up in connection with a few crimes we're investigating. We're keen to talk to him, if only to eliminate him from our enquiries."

"Ah, I see." The woman took a sip from the mug sitting on the side table next to her. "It's a bit cold now. Would you like a drink of something while you're here?"

Hero raised a hand. "No thanks, Mrs. Taylor. I wondered if you could tell me if you've heard Foster receive any visitors lately? Perhaps in the last couple of weeks?"

"I hear all sorts coming from there all the time, what with the blasted walls being paper thin. These old flats could do with being pulled down, but there's little chance of that happening. Not enough housing for folks like me around these parts anyway, is there?"

"I'm sorry you have to live with such an inconvenience. Perhaps the council will sort you out a new place soon."

"They might consider it, if the likes of you put in a good word for me?" The woman's chubby cheeks flushed a little when she smiled and aimed a cheeky wink at Hero.

Not again! "If only I had such clout. Sadly, I don't. I'm a mere DI who rarely gets listened to by authority on such important life-changing matters. So, can you tell us if Foster has had any visitors lately?"

"A woman was here last week. Don't go asking me what day it was, because when you get to my age, one day goes into the next. I tend to live for the day my pension comes round. All the other days simply pass me by."

"I take it pension day is on a Thursday?"

"That's right, dear. I see what you did there, very clever. Yes, I remember I heard raised voices coming from next door on Friday night, I believe it was. Does that help any?" She smiled at him again, pleased with the spark of memory she'd just shaken free.

"Excellent. If I showed you a photo of a woman we think might have visited Foster in the past, would that help?"

"Only if I was outside when she arrived at his place. As you can see, I haven't got any windows at the front of the flat, only at the back, and that ain't a pretty sight, either. The only reason I knew you were out there today was because I heard you knock on his door and call out his name. Oh, and the fact that you announced you were the police. I wouldn't have opened the door if I hadn't heard that. You never know who's likely to bump you on the head nowadays, do you?"

"It's better to be safe, that's for sure, Mrs. Taylor. Now, what do you think of this?" Hero held out the ten-by-eight photograph of Cathy Daws.

The woman looked at the picture from all angles. "I wouldn't like to say, really. I suppose she looks like a woman I saw knocking on his door about a month ago. Not sure, though. That day, I had just come back from the shop down below, probably been out for a pint of milk. That's the only thing I tend to buy downstairs. Run by Indians, it is, and they take advantage of us old folks. Every month, my daughter pops by to take me shopping at that big Tesco on the edge of town. Oops… sorry. I'm off again, ain't I? Don't be afraid to tell me to shut up. I get very few visitors, you see. It's nice to have a bit of company now and again. Are you sure you wouldn't like a cup of tea?"

"I understand, and no, thank you. You're very kind. Well, that's promising that you think you've seen this person here. It contradicts what the woman has already intimated. So you've done well there. What about men? Does he get many male visitors? Do you know?"

"Let me think… maybe one or two over the last month or so."

Hero handed the woman the photo of Stuart Daws. She went through the same ritual of studying the picture from different angles before she shook her head. "Sorry, can't say I recognise that one."

"Not to worry. This is the last one, then we'll get out of your hair." He passed her Lomax's photo.

Mrs. Taylor recognised the man immediately. She started waving the photo around then stabbed at it with her gnarled arthritic finger. "Yes, now this one I'm sure about. I think he was here awhile back."

Hero glanced at Julie, his eyes widening with expectation. "How long? A week, two weeks, a month even?"

"Oh, now that, I'm a bit fuzzy about. Maybe a good month or so, I would imagine. Why? What's he done? What have they both been up to? I'm dying to know?"

"Again, that's really helpful. Honestly, it's pure speculation right now."

"Hey, if I've got murderers hanging around here or something like that, I think I have a right to know."

Hero cringed. He really didn't want to scare the old woman. However, he did think she had a right to know if she was in any immediate danger. "I don't want to worry you. At this moment, your neighbour is just wanted for questioning in a robbery case and a suspicious death."

The woman's mouth dropped open. "Bloody hell, I was only joking about the murderer thing. Right, the second you leave I'm going to get onto that bloomin' council and demand a move. How am I supposed to sleep at night now, knowing that I could be living next door to a bloody murderer? Good heavens above, my Bert would be doing somersaults in his grave if he thought I was in mortal danger like that."

"Honestly, Mrs. Taylor, I think you're overreacting. We've got several teams on the lookout for Foster. I doubt very much he'll come back here anytime soon. Hopefully, we'll pick him up before long. Perhaps you should consider staying with your daughter for the next week or so. What do you think?"

The woman looked around the room. "I know this doesn't look much to you, but it's all I've got. This is my home, and I'll be damned if I'm going to be driven from it, under any circumstances. I'll be fine here, providing you lot do your job correctly and catch the bastard. Anyway, me and the son-in-law don't exactly get on. I'd only be in the way if I stayed with them. It would only pile added stress on their already-stressful marriage."

"I totally understand. You have my word we'll do all we can to protect you. Be sure to keep your door locked and bolted at all times, and if someone should knock on your door, get them to post their ID through the letterbox for you to see, all right?"

Mrs. Taylor stood up to show them to the front door. "Now there's no need to preach, sonny. I've lived, without incident, by myself for five years now. I'll be fine, I hope," she quietly added the final two words as an afterthought.

"Thanks for helping today. Stay safe. We'll do all we can to help you on that front, too." Hero smiled, then he and Julie walked out of the flat.

"Shall we keep trying?" Julie asked. "There are a few more flats to consider. Any visitors Foster had would need to pass them to get to his."

"Yep, let's split up. You go that way, and I'll try this one here."

Julie knocked on the door to the left of Foster's flat, but there was no answer. Hero received the same result on the next two doors he tried. In the end, they gave up and returned to the station.

* * *

Stan Foster's heart pounded as he watched the two suited people he presumed were detectives leave his building. *Damn, that rules out trying to get back into the flat for a change of clothes anytime soon.* He sniffed his underarm and recoiled at the smell. He hadn't washed or changed clothes in days. Normally, that wouldn't bother him, but the fact that the awkward situation he found himself in was making him sweat more than usual made his need to change clothes all the more urgent.

He shielded himself behind the industrial-sized metal wheelie bins and waited until the detectives' car passed before he took out his phone and placed the call. Had he been right to ring the detective like that? Had they traced his call? *What other reason would the police have to come here and see me?*

He pressed the number one and listened to the dial tone for what seemed like an eternity. Eventually, the person he was after answered the phone.

"Yes, what do you want, Stan?"

"You gotta help me."

The woman let out a derisory laugh. "I do! Who says?"

"Come on, I need a place to stay. You bloody got me in this mess. It's the least you can do."

She laughed again. "Get stuffed. No one forced you to do what you've done. Why can't you stay at your flat?"

"Because the filth have just been there. How do they know where I live?"

"It's not difficult to find out. Surely, you have a mate who'll help you out. Go and kip on their floor for a day or two until everything settles down."

"I've got no mates. Stuart was my mate. Now he's gone, I've got no one I can rely on," Stan whined out of frustration.

"You'll have to hide out in your car, then, won't you? You're definitely not welcome here. The cops could come knocking on my door at any time. Anyway, I'm busy," she replied curtly.

Stan searched around him. Did he dare try to make it up to his flat? He shook his head. That would be like committing suicide. Maybe it would be better to leave it a few days before he tried to get in there to retrieve fresh clothes.

"All right, thanks for nothing. I've got a word of warning for you."

"Yeah, what's that?"

"If I go down for what's happened, I'll be taking you with me. I ain't taking the rap for any fucker. Have you got that?"

"You can try and take me with you, but we both know I've covered my tracks well in all of this," the woman retorted before she ended the call.

Stan was left seething. She was right. *How the heck did I get so involved in this?* He ran back to his car in a crouched position, relieved that the detectives hadn't spotted his vehicle in the car park of one of the shops. He started the engine and sat there for a while, having no idea where he could drive to next for the shelter he desperately needed. He pulled away and headed into the country, where he would be less likely to be discovered.

CHAPTER TEN

That evening, Hero returned home feeling dissatisfied by the day's lack of progress. He had hoped that the case would have found some traction and even a forward momentum. But nothing could be further from the truth.

"Hi, Fay," he knelt beside his wife, who was nursing one of the twins on the couch, and kissed her cheek. "Good day? Did the girls behave themselves?"

"Not bad. A few niggles here and there. I suppose I'll need to get used to that. Double the trouble and all that. You've got a visitor." Fay nodded her head at the person standing behind him, leaning in the doorway of the kitchen.

"Sis? What are you doing here?" Hero asked, surprised to see Cara.

Fay nudged him with her foot. "Take it in the kitchen, guys, will you. I don't want the little ones picking up on any bad vibes."

Hero stood and frowned at his wife. "Bad vibes? Why would there be bad vibes when I'm talking to my sister?"

"You haven't heard her news yet." Fay winked and looked down at Zara.

Hero ran a worried hand over his face as he stepped into the kitchen to switch on the kettle. Looking anxious, Cara sat at the kitchen table, her hands clenched tightly together. He didn't say anything until he'd made two very strong coffees and sat down opposite her. Cara grabbed her mug and wrapped her hands around it.

"Okay, let's have it. Are you pregnant?"

His sister's head shot up, and their gazes locked. "No, I am *not*! Christ, if only that was the case, do you think I'd be crapping myself like this?"

Hero leaned back in his chair and braced himself. "All right. So what's wrong then? Come on, hon. I would like to spend some time with my family this evening, if that's okay with you?"

Cara's chair scraped back, and she stood up. "Sorry to have disturbed your evening, I'll come back another time."

Hero ducked down to get in her sightline. Searching her eyes, he cursed himself for being so abrupt towards her when he saw the tears welling up in his twin's eyes. "Cara, what's wrong? You're starting to worry me now. Forget my crass remark. Sit down and tell me. I'm always willing to share your troubles. You know that."

Cara slumped into her chair and buried her shaking head in her hands.

Hero shot out of his own chair to comfort her. "Sweetheart, you're seriously beginning to worry me." He had to wait until her out-of-character sobbing ceased before he could try again. "Sis, tell me what's happened?"

Cara wiped the drips from her nose on her sleeve, making Hero cringe. "I did something stupid."

That much, Hero had already assumed. "Such as?"

She inhaled a large breath and let it out slowly before she replied, "I hit someone."

Hero was tempted to laugh, but he restrained himself because he sensed Cara was about to follow up with something far more substantial than hitting someone. "And?"

"It just happened to be my instructor."

Hero covered his face with his hand and groaned. "Tell me you're joking?"

"I'm not. Don't go all high and mighty on me now. He had it coming. He has WHT."

"What? WHT?"

"Wandering hand trouble. He never knows when to keep his hands to himself. The other girls might not mind him having a sneaky grope when no one's looking, but I bloody do!"

"Cara, Cara, Cara… what have you done?"

She pushed her mug away in disgust. "Well, I thought I'd get support from you, at least."

"Of course I'll support you. It doesn't alter the fact that your fiery temper has probably caused severe damage to your career and got you thrown off the course."

"Why is it always my fault? He groped me *first*. Doesn't that effing count for anything?" Cara leaned forward and lowered her voice in case Louie overheard them talking. "Why do men always think we women should ignore such assaults? If you men didn't think with that thing dangling between your legs ninety percent of the time, this type of shit wouldn't happen."

"You're twisting my words, and you know it. No, no woman should ever ignore harassment of that or any other kind. However, these issues have to take the right route in order for things to change. You thrashing out like that has only made your situation a darn sight worse."

"Gee thanks! Just what I want to hear."

"You know what I'm getting at. I shouldn't have to point out the obvious. You're not stupid. Were there any witnesses?"

"Witnesses? What to? His assault or mine?"

"Both, preferably the former. Well?" Hero took a sip of his coffee then pushed Cara's mug back across the table to within her reach.

"Yes, but everyone I've talked to is denying it," she replied glumly.

"Jesus, really? I see there's a lot of solidarity within your group then."

"Ha, hardly. The girls are shitting themselves after seeing me instantly suspended."

"Crap. Do you want me to see if I can find out what's going on?"

"There's no point. This instructor has been at the training centre for years. Who are the disciplinary panel likely to believe, him or me?"

"Who is the instructor, and what did he actually do?"

"His name is Wade. He was using me as a willing participant in a self-defence class."

Hero raised a hand. "Are you sure you haven't misconstrued anything, Cara?"

"Jesus, Hero, give me some credit, will you? The guy groped my breast, for Christ's sake. Why the hell would he bloody need to do that?"

"All right, don't bite my head off. I'm merely trying to figure out what's gone on and how we can offer up some kind of defence."

"Sorry. Can't you understand how frustrating all of this is for me? You're lucky. You men don't have to put up with shit like this."

"Granted, there have only been a few cases of sexual assault brought against an ex-instructor that I know of. We have to be one hundred percent sure before we fight back on this one, Cara. A man's career could hang in the balance here."

"Hero! I can't believe you just said that. What about my effing career? Doesn't that count in all of this? Why do you think I'm so upset?"

"It does. You know it does. I'm just saying that we have to be cautious how we tackle the authorities. Obviously, it would be better if you had witnesses who were willing to speak up for you, but if there aren't any, then I sense that we're in for a tough ride." He reached across the table and squeezed her hand tightly. "You know that I'll be behind you one hundred percent, love, even if that means putting my own career in jeopardy."

"I can't ask you to do that. If you get involved, the higher-ups will just take it that you're up to your old tricks again, out to cause trouble."

"No they won't. I've behaved myself in that department for the past few years now. My disciplinary record shouldn't be called into question. I'm concerned about you, not me, though. Most of the time, if a recruit is put on suspension, then their career usually comes to a grinding halt."

"Yeah, that's what I thought. That's my biggest concern in all of this. Should I consider just walking away?"

Hero thought while he took another sip from his mug. "That's a tough call and one that ultimately, you'll have to make. In my book, the force would be foolish to lose you. And if you walk away from the training, I think it could turn out to be the biggest mistake of your life."

"So what's the answer?"

"I'm thinking." Hero smiled, hoping it would be infectious. It wasn't.

"Well, think faster. I'm drowning fast, brother dearest."

"Knock, knock, mind if we come in?" Fay asked from the doorway. Little Louie had his arms wrapped around her legs, and she was still holding Zara.

"I think you'll need to get rid of your hanger-on if you intend coming in." He laughed and rose from his seat to lend his wife a hand. "Here, let me take my beautiful daughter."

"Thanks, that's a great help. Someone not far from here wants his hot chocolate before going to bed. Don't you, mate?" Fay ruffled her son's hair, and he let go of her legs and ran to the fridge to retrieve the milk carton.

Hero glanced at his watch. "God, is it that time already? I don't know where the time goes."

Cara stood and looked at Hero and Fay. "I'm sorry for taking up so much of your valuable time. I'll leave you to it now."

"You will not. Sit down. We haven't finished yet, and stop taking umbrage just because I told the truth about the time." He turned to Fay. "We've got enough dinner for Cara to join us, haven't we, love? I can ring for a takeaway or chop a few extra veggies."

"I don't mind. It's up to Cara."

"No need, I think I'd rather go anyway. I want to try and get my head around a few things. I appreciate the advice, Hero. Maybe I'll ring you later for another chat if things refuse to become clearer."

Hero stepped forward and kissed his sister on the cheek. "We're behind you, love. Don't ever doubt that. You don't have to leave. I'd rather you stayed and discussed it once the little one's ears are out of earshot."

"Thanks. I've made up my mind. I think I need a drink to help me decide what to do next. I'll call at the pub on the way home."

"Well, you know my answer to that. Drink never solved anything, love. I should know. I used to be a walking pint of beer, remember?" He smiled again, hoping to lighten the atmosphere a little.

"I'll talk later. I promise I won't get bladdered, despite needing to." Cara picked up her jacket and handbag and left the house.

Fay ran a hand down Hero's arm and kissed the top of her daughter's head. "Did you manage to get anywhere with her? No, before you answer that, let's get this young man sorted and tucked up in bed first."

After giving Louie his treat and bathing him together, Hero and Fay collapsed onto the couch with a glass of orange juice. Because of Hero's past drinking problems, that was really all he allowed to pass his lips nowadays, maybe an odd pint down the pub with his work colleagues after they'd successfully closed a case, but certainly nothing more than that.

Fay tucked her legs up onto the couch beside him and placed her head on his chest. "Do you want to talk about Cara?"

"I think we should. I take it she told you what had happened?"

Fay sighed and caressed his hand. "It's not a situation I would envy getting caught up in."

"And if that had occurred with you, how would you have dealt with it, Fay?"

"I don't think anyone could answer that properly until they found themselves in that kind of difficulty. But I certainly would have struck out if it did happen to me. I have, in fact."

Hero placed his glass on the table next to him and pushed Fay upright so he could look into her eyes. "When? Where? Why didn't you tell me?"

"Hey, stop with all the questions. The incident took place when I first started work. I didn't even know you back then. Some sleazy guy in the packing department at a factory I used to work at. I only lasted there a week, and the job was just too mundane for words. Anyway, he copped a feel of my backside one day when I was stretching over the conveyor belt to get something. The rest of the workforce thought it was hilarious until I kneed the little shit in the groin. He ended up putting in a complaint about me."

"Geez, the gall of some people. What did your boss do?"

"Sacked me."

"Sacked you! Why?"

"Men tend to stick together at times like this, Hero. Maybe it's a male ego thing. I don't know."

"That's despicable. What reason did the boss give for sacking you?" Hero asked, shaking his head in disgust.

"I wasn't up to scratch. I was just within my seven-day trial period, which by the way, I never even knew existed. So as the bloke who assaulted me had been there for donkey's years, they took his word over mine."

"But you had a bunch of witnesses."

"Yep, all of them friendly with him."

Hero inhaled and let the breath escape slowly through tight lips. "Were there any female witnesses?"

"At least ten of them. My take on it is that they had gone through a similar experience. Maybe it was some kind of initiation test. If you didn't retaliate or squeal to the boss, then you got accepted. That was my reading of the situation, anyway. Of course, no one would agree with my assumption. I suppose they thought if they spoke out in my favour, their jobs would be on the line, too."

"I've never even considered this sort of thing before. Do you think it's prevalent in all trades and workplaces?"

"I'm not sure. I'd say about fifty percent. I dread to think how many women out there never speak out about the harassment they receive at work. You only have to look at the statistics surrounding rape. You know how many women are too scared to come forward to the police, right? Well, it would be the same in this instance, surely. I have no doubt about that, Hero. Meanwhile, scum like Cara's instructor get away with it time and time again."

"We'll see about that." He reached for his glass and took a sip.

"Now don't go doing anything silly. I recognise that look."

He pointed a finger at his chest. "Are you talking to me? Would I?"

Fay kissed him on the lips before resting her head on his chest again. "If you have to get involved, be careful. In my experience, men who carry out this so-called 'innocent fun crimes' can be a force to be reckoned with."

"Yeah, and so can I be once I'm angered. Wade will get what's coming to him."

CHAPTER ELEVEN

The bright sunlight hurt Hero's eyes on the drive into work the following morning. Added to his sleep deprivation because of the twins' incessant crying all night, he feared he was in for a long, arduous day. During his sleepless night, his mind had constantly mulled over his sister's predicament, and he'd finally come up with a plan to help Cara out.

He put his foot down and pulled into the car park just as Foxy was parking her car. He papped his horn, intimating that he wanted her to wait for him.

"Morning, Foxy."

"Morning, sir. Rough night with the kids?" She smiled and locked her car.

He bent down and looked at himself in the wing mirror of her car. "Christ," he moaned, "is it that obvious?"

"Afraid so."

"I'd like a quick chat if I may. It's a personal matter."

She raised her hand in front of her. "If it's about babies, forget it. I wouldn't have a clue in that department."

He snorted. "No, it's not. You might think I'm being a little cheeky here, but Cara is in a heap of trouble, not of her doing, well... sort of. Anyway, I've promised I'll do all I can to help her."

"Sounds ominous. Are you going to tell me what kind of trouble your sister is in, or do I have to guess?"

"Sorry, I was getting around to it, honest." Hero relayed the conversation he'd had with Cara the previous night.

Foxy looked perplexed. "Bloody hell! She doesn't believe in doing things by halves, does she? I'm puzzled how you think I can be of help, sir."

"Well, here's the sneaky part. I need to find some dirt I can fling at this instructor. You know as well as I do that there's no point looking through his work background. It's sure to be cleaner than a pair of nun's knickers."

"All right, I hear what you're saying, but I'm still lost about how I can help, sir. Sorry for being so dense. In my defence, it is first thing."

"My fault, my brain's running ahead of my mouth, as usual. Well, I thought you might have a quiet word with your hubby for me?"

"Frank? I'm still not with you, sir."

"He's bound to have come across some dirt on this guy. Your hubby always has his ear pressed firmly to the ground. Would you mind asking him if he knows anything about Julian Wade's reputation with the ladies, maybe? Let's put it that way, shall we?"

"Ahh… I'm with you. I can certainly try. I would do that now, only Frank's been out undercover all night. When we passed on the doorstep this morning, he was on his way to crash into bed. He looked done in, to be honest, sir."

"There's no rush. Not for a few hours at least. What time does he usually get up?"

"Around two or three. I could ring him then, if you like?"

"Thanks, Foxy, I'd like to get the ball well and truly rolling on this one as soon as possible. My sister's whole career is on the line because of this sick tosser."

Foxy winked. "If there's a way of dealing with this guy, I'm sure we can come up with something concrete between us, sir."

"That's what I was hoping. Right, let's get back to the other frustrating cases cluttering up our schedule, eh?"

They walked into the incident room together, and Hero immediately looked over at his partner's empty desk. Frowning, he asked Jason, "Julie not around yet?"

"She's rung in sick, sir. Apparently, her mother's health went downhill during the night. Julie said she wanted to be there when she passed over."

"Christ, it's that bad? Poor Julie. I'll ring her this evening to find out how she's dealing with things."

"Yes, sir."

Hero stopped at Foxy's desk on his way through to tackle his morning paperwork. "On second thoughts, pertaining to our discussion, do a quick background check on Wade this morning, if you would? Plus, I want you to be ready to go at a moment's notice if we get called out. You'll be standing in for Julie today, all right?"

"Brilliant, I mean, thanks, sir. Poor Julie. I hope she's coping okay. I'll do the necessary checks now and get back to you ASAP."

"Good girl. I'll be in my office." He tapped her desktop as he walked away. "Lance, join me for a minute, will you?" Hero called out. He put a couple of coins in the vending machine and ordered a strong black coffee.

DS Powell knocked on his door and walked into the small office a few seconds later. "Yes, boss?"

"Don't look so worried, man. Or should I say, what are you looking so worried about? You look as guilty as sin."

"Sorry, sir, didn't mean to. Nope, I haven't done anything wrong, not that I can put my finger on."

"Sit down." Hero removed the lid from his paper cup and sipped his coffee, regretting not leaving the drink to cool down for a while before drinking it. "Crap, I expected that to be cooler!"

Lance sat opposite him and folded his arms. "What's up, boss?"

"I've been thinking over the case. Foster is going to be the key to all this. I think we should set up a surveillance unit outside his flat."

"Good idea. Who did you have in mind for the job, sir?"

Hero grinned. "Funny you should ask that. I thought you and Jason could do it."

Lance unfolded his arms and rose from his chair. "I don't mind. You want us out there now?"

"Why not? There's nothing more we can do on the case until we find Foster. I'll get in touch with uniform, make sure they've still got his vehicle on the priority list."

"Roger that. I'll grab Jason and get out there. How long do you want us casing his joint for? All day?" Lance said, imitating a character from one of his favourite American cop shows.

Hero smiled. "And into the evening, if you have to. I'll drop by the super's office and sanction some overtime. I guess I should have checked if that's okay with you first. You haven't got any pressing personal commitments booked for this evening, have you?"

"Not me, I'm good to go. I'll check with Jason. He's an eager pup. I'm sure he'll be willing to drop anything he has planned, sir."

"Good. Check in periodically, will you? We'll see how the day progresses as to how long you guys stay out there. I don't have to tell you to park discreetly, do I?"

"No, sir. Right, we'll be off, then, if there's nothing else?"

"Stay safe and out of sight. Check in around lunchtime, okay, Lance?"

"Yes, sir."

As Hero had anticipated first thing that morning, the day turned out to be exceptionally long. The rest of the team, namely Foxy, worked her butt off without achieving very much at all. She reported back to him just after lunch that her husband Frank would be making some subtle enquiries about Wade. Despite searching his background, Foxy hadn't stumbled across anything worthwhile on record pointing to Wade's questionable behaviour towards his pupils.

After checking in with the surveillance team, Hero went home, in the hope that he would be able to spend some time with his family.

Louie ran into his arms the second Hero stepped through the front door. "Daddy, welcome home. Come play Xbox with me?"

"Give me a chance to get in the door, tiger. Have you been good for mummy today?"

"Of course." Louie wriggled out of his arms and ran back into the lounge. "Mummy, Daddy's home."

Hero walked into the kitchen and gathered Fay in his arms. "How were the girls today?"

"Zonked out most of the day. I hope we don't suffer again tonight. You look exhausted, love."

"So do you. And there I was thinking people were just pulling my leg when they said double the trouble when referring to having twins. Did you manage to catch forty winks today?"

"Not really. Did you?" Fay laughed.

He kissed the tip of her nose. "Between you and me, I think I managed to drop off once or twice during my paperwork chores this morning. If it hadn't been for the guys ringing to check in with me, I think I'd still be at the office, sound asleep."

"Checking in about what?" Fay twisted out of his clutches and stirred the bolognaise sauce bubbling and splattering on the hob.

"I've posted a couple of guys outside a suspect's house. They're going to be there all evening. I've told them to call me before they finish their shift. I hope that's all right?"

"Of course it is. I know how important this case is and that you wouldn't do that ordinarily. I'm about to serve up. Can you do your fatherly duties and ensure Louie has washed his hands properly before we eat?"

Hero kissed her cheek and pinched her on the backside.

"Oi, you! Do you want a sexual harassment charge landing on the doormat?"

"Christ, don't even joke about things like that. I've got Foxy's husband on Cara's case. He works in Vice. Frank comes across this type of shit all the time regarding dodgy officers. He'll be reporting back in a few days."

"That's great, hon. Don't go raising your hopes, though, will you? We all know what kind of cover-ups go on in the Met. Now… son… hands… washing!"

"All right, sorry." He went through to the lounge and extracted the game console from Louie's sweaty palms. "Time for dinner, son. We're under orders to get cleaned up. I'll race you to the bathroom."

Father and son ran upstairs amidst squeals, joyful laughter, and the sound of Sammy's playful barking as he chased them.

After enjoying a fulfilling bolognaise and pasta dinner followed by a scrummy, gooey chocolate fudge dessert, Hero cleared up the kitchen and dropped onto the couch alongside Fay for five minutes before he started the evening ritual of putting Louie to bed.

* * *

"Yeah, it's me again," Stan Foster said when she picked up the phone.

"What the hell do you want? I'm bloody regretting giving you my mobile number now. I'm at work, and I'm bloody busy."

"I didn't know who else to call. I've got no one else. Shit, don't cut me off like this. You owe me. You hear me? The least you can do is be there for when I need someone to sound off to. You got me into this mess. I can't cope out here on the streets. I'm going back to the flat, screw the consequences."

"Like I give a shit. Go back to the flat if you want. Just stop hassling me. Got it?"

"Has anyone ever told you what a cold-hearted bitch you can be?"

"Yep, all the time. You knew what you were getting into when you met me. Now's not the time to be whining and bawling your eyes out. Get a life and man up."

Foster was left staring at the phone when she hung up on him. Furious, he crept along the shadows close to the shops and ran up the concrete stairs to his flat above, hoping none of the neighbours came outside before he was tucked safely away inside his flat. He felt sure the neighbours would be on the lookout for him, eager to ring the police with news of his reappearance, especially the old dear next door. He quietly let himself in and gently secured the door behind him, making sure that the old girl next door couldn't hear a pin drop through the glass he suspected she kept affixed to the wall. All he needed was a change of clothes. He'd have to forget taking a shower since his bathroom was located next to the party wall. A quick strip-down wash would have to suffice. He left his clothes in a heap on the bedroom floor and lifted the mattress to retrieve the few hundred pounds he kept for emergencies.

After taking one final look around the bedroom for anything he might have forgotten, he turned to go back in the lounge. His breath caught, and he froze in the doorway.

"You? What are you doing here?" he asked, forgetting to lower his voice to avoid alerting his neighbour.

"I felt guilty and thought I'd drop by to lend you a hand."

"But you said you were at work. You made your position perfectly clear. I get it—you've used me. There's no need for us to see each other again, to extend this so-called 'friendship.' You shouldn't have come here. We're through."

She sauntered across the floor towards him, a sexy smile set firmly in place.

"You can pack that in. That kind of behaviour might have worked on me in the beginning, but not anymore." He reached out for her shoulders with the intention of turning her and pushing her towards the front door. However, he spotted the knife she was holding at the very last moment.

CHAPTER TWELVE

Hero and Fay kissed and shared a rare cuddle on the couch, but Hero's ringing phone disturbed them.

He groaned an apology and untangled himself to answer it on the third ring. "Hello. DI Nelson."

"Hello, dear. This is Mrs. Taylor. You came to see me today. Do you remember? I live in the flats above the shops."

Hero sat forward in his seat, concerned by the fear emanating from the woman's voice. "Of course I remember. Is everything all right, Mrs. Taylor?"

"I'm sorry to disturb you, but you told me to ring you if I heard anything next door. Well, I've just heard voices and a large thud. Not sure what the heck that was."

"Okay, just sit tight. I'll get someone there right away. Thanks for informing me. Keep your door shut and stay in your flat at all times, all right?"

"Yes, dear. Oh, my, please hurry."

"I'm on my way."

Hero hung up and raced around the room, searching for his jacket and shoes while he dialled another number. "Jason. Are you still at the location?"

"Yes, boss. We were just about to call it a day and ring you, but you beat me to it."

"Have you seen anyone lurking around?"

"No, boss. It's been pretty dull here all day."

"Stay there. I'm on my way. I've just had a call from the next-door neighbour, saying she thought she'd heard a noise coming from inside the flat. Voices and then a thud. We'll investigate the flat together. I'll be ten minutes at the most. Wait at the bottom of the stairs for me. Make sure no one leaves the area, okay?"

"Yes, boss. We'll get into position now."

Hero kissed Fay. "I'm sorry, love. I've gotta run. Don't wait up."

"Go. I understand. Ring me if you can. Drive carefully, sweetheart."

"I will," he called out in a hushed voice from the front door.

Hero jumped in the car and put his foot down. He arrived at the flats around eight minutes later to find Jason and Lance waiting for him at the bottom of the stairs. "Has anyone left the area?"

"No, boss." Jason and Lance shook their heads.

"Let's get in there. Be prepared for a scrap, lads."

They crept up the stairs and along the corridor to Foster's flat. The front door was ajar, and Hero eased it open. *This looks ominous.*

He tilted his head, listening for any tell-tale signs of movement for a second or two before he motioned for his men to follow him into the depths of the flat. His pace picked up when Hero saw a man lying prostrate on the lounge floor, a large kitchen knife sticking out of his chest. "Quick, call an ambulance."

Lance stepped outside to make the call to avoid the reception fluctuating during the emergency.

"Sir. Foster, can you hear me?" Hero searched around for a cushion or something soft he could use as a prop under the man's head. "Look in the bathroom for some towels, Jason. We've got to stop the bleeding."

Jason darted out of the room. Hero grabbed the holdall sitting on the sofa and pulled out several of the man's jumpers, which he placed under the injured man's head to stop him from potentially choking on his blood. The man moaned with each movement but said nothing.

Hero tried again. "Foster, blink your eyes if you can hear me."

Foster's eyes fluttered to a close then opened slightly again as he tried to blink in response.

"Can you tell me who did this?"

Foster let out another groan, but his parched lips failed to form any audible words.

"Jesus, where the hell is that ambulance? Jason, put the towels around the wound. Don't touch that knife, for God's sake."

The young DC looked panic-stricken. "Which wound? There's quite a few of them? Never mind, I'll cover what I can."

"Good man. This was quite a frenzied attack. Look at the blood spatter on the walls. Keep stemming the blood flow. I'll call the station and get SOCO out here."

Hero stood up and left the flat. He pulled in a large breath of fresh air before ringing the station. He knew the importance of getting the investigation into the crime scene rolling at the earliest opportunity in such a case.

He returned to the flat when he heard the wailing siren and spotted the paramedics drawing into the car park below. "How's he doing, Jason?"

"Not good, sir."

"Get ready to stand aside when the paramedics arrive. We don't want to hamper them in any way."

A uniformed man and woman entered the lounge, carrying a padded emergency bag and a stretcher.

"He's fading, guys. We need to get him out of here and en route to the hospital as quickly as possible," Hero said, his heart pounding.

"Let us do our job, sir. Stand back please?" the male paramedic instructed. He dropped to his knees to assess Foster's injuries for himself. Then he ordered his partner to rig up the oxygen while he issued a pain-killing injection to the patient. "Let's do what we can and get this man out of here within five minutes, June, all right?"

The female paramedic nodded and searched in the bag for the items she needed. Then she stood up and quickly assembled the stretcher, snapping the catches into place to ensure it didn't collapse under the patient's weight.

"Anything I can do?" Hero asked, feeling like a spare part at a wedding, his hands nervously darting in and out of his pockets.

The male paramedic glanced up at him. "We might need a hand getting the stretcher down the stairs in a few moments. Other than that, we're good, thanks."

"No problem. Just shout when you need us."

Foster moaned when the female paramedic raised his head to attach the oxygen mask over his mouth and nose. A short while later, the male paramedic announced that they were ready to move the casualty onto the stretcher.

"As gently as we can, folks. One, two, and lift."

Hero, Jason, and the two paramedics lifted the injured man onto the metal stretcher. Foster's moaning intensified but subsided a little once he was securely strapped in. The team moved swiftly. Hero ordered his two men to remain at the scene until the forensic team arrived and gave them permission to knock off once they handed the reins over, while Hero helped the paramedics down the stairs and into the ambulance. Then he followed the speeding ambulance in his own vehicle to the Salford Royal Hospital. On the way, Hero rang Fay to update her on what had taken place and told her not to expect him any time soon.

The paramedics wheeled Foster through to the Accident and Emergency department. A doctor told Hero to wait outside the room while he and the nursing staff did their best to save the patient in their expert care. Hero paced up and down for the next ten minutes or so, until the doctor finally came to update him on Foster's condition.

"DI Nelson, I'm Dr. Jenkins. We've managed to stem the bleeding. He'll be taken down to surgery to remove the knife once the emergency theatre team has been assembled. Did you want a word with him before he goes down to theatre? Because to be truthful, he only has a slim chance of pulling through."

"If I could. Has he said anything?"

The doctor shook his head. "Not at all. He's heavily sedated now, so I doubt you're going to get much out of him."

"Thanks. I just want a name, that's all. Can I go in?"

"Let's get him moved into a cubicle first." The doctor walked back into the examination room and returned to the corridor a few seconds later, accompanied by an orderly, who was guiding Foster's bed into a nearby cubicle. Holding back the curtain, the doctor beckoned Hero to step forward. "Try and be gentle with him."

"Of course I will, Doc." Hero leaned over the patient, close enough to hear any response coming from the man's dry lips. "Mr. Foster, can you tell me who did this to you?"

Foster swallowed and parted his lips slightly.

"Go on, just one name if that's all you can manage for now. We'll get more from you after the surgery."

His tongue moistened his lips, and he turned his head in slow motion to face Hero.

"Yes, go on, say the name?"

His lips moved as if he were going to speak. Then they went slack as another bout of pain shot through him.

"Please try, Mr. Foster?"

"One more minute, and then I'll have to ask you to leave, Inspector. You can see the patient is struggling to speak."

"I know. Let me try one more time?" He lowered his ear to the man's lips and asked the same question. "Mr. Foster, please give me a name? Who did this to you?"

He received only a gurgling breath in return.

Then Hero asked, "Mr. Foster, what can you tell me about Stuart Daws's murder?"

Still nothing.

"What about Mark Lomax? Did you know him? Did you know either man?"

Finally, Foster gave a brief nod and made a weak attempt to speak.

Hero lowered his ear to the patient's face.

"C... Ca..." That was Foster's final word before the last painful breath left his body.

"Mr. Foster, please? What are you trying to say?" Hero asked out of desperation.

The doctor placed a hand on Hero's arm and steered him out of the cubicle, into the hallway. "I'm sorry. Go home, Inspector. There's nothing more you can do here."

Hero's shoulders slumped, and he staggered back against the wall. "He was just about to tell me who the murderer was."

"Do you have any suspects beginning with 'Ca'?" the doctor asked sympathetically.

Hero launched himself off the wall and shook the doctor's hand. "Yes, I do. Thanks, Doc. Sorry you lost a patient."

"Sorry you gained a victim. I hope you find the culprit soon."

Hero was already racing along the hallway to the car park when he called back over his shoulder, "I think we'll have this case wrapped up in no time at all. Thanks, Doc."

CHAPTER THIRTEEN

Instead of jumping in and arresting Cathy Daws straight away, Hero managed to restrain himself, insisting that it would be better to tackle the woman the following day, after everything settled down and seemed much clearer. Without any actual hard evidence, he knew it would be wrong to arrest the woman immediately. The Crown Prosecution Services would laugh at his request anyway.

At work, he gathered his team while he added the latest victim to the evidence board. "Sadly, Stan Foster lost his life after receiving a fatal wound to the chest. The knife must have nicked his heart. Despite the doctors doing their best, there was little they could do to pull him through. Here's the interesting part. I was with him when he died. As he took a final breath, he tried to tell me his attacker's name." He turned to face the board and tapped one of the photos with his pen. "I believe it's none other than Cathy Daws." Some of the team gasped, while others simply nodded their unsurprised acceptance. "Actually, all he said was 'Ca…' but you don't have to have a brilliant mind to figure out who he was getting at, do you?"

"So, are we going to arrest her, sir?" Foxy jumped in quickly.

"Not until we have some solid evidence, Foxy. I'm going to ring the pathologist this morning to see if he'll prioritise his team's findings from Foster's flat. If this woman can be connected to all three crimes, then we should be able to throw the net over her soon."

"Can we put her under some kind of surveillance, sir?" Jason asked, resting his hand under his chin in a thoughtful pose.

Hero clicked his fingers. "That was going to be my next suggestion. Jason, do me a favour and ring the landlord of the Dog and Duck. Steve Gillan, I believe his name is? Ask him if Cathy Daws was at work last night, all night, okay?"

"Yes, boss." Jason went back to his desk and picked up the phone. Before long, he returned to the group with the news Hero least expected to hear. "Sorry, sir. Mr. Gillan says that she was behind the bar all evening. 'Every minute of the evening' were his exact words."

"What? How the hell can that be? This is another reason we can't go barging in there to arrest the woman. Her alibis are always of the concrete variety." He glanced at the board again. "Two murders that we think we can pin on Cathy Daws, her husband and Foster, and yet both times, she has an alibi of working at the pub. How can that be?"

"Maybe we should start investigating this Gillan bloke, the landlord?" Lance offered, nudging Jason to back him up.

Hero furrowed his brow. "You might be on to something there, Powell. Just to be clear on this, you and Jason are sure you never saw Cathy arrive at the scene last night, during your surveillance of the flat?"

Both detectives shook their heads.

"Well, that's weird, isn't it? You didn't drop off to sleep, did you?"

Jason pulled his shoulders back and shook his head vigorously. "No, sir, we did not. I can't tell you how many times I've gone over this during the night. None of it makes sense."

"All right, I believe you. Jason, do the background checks on the landlord?"

"Yes, boss. I'll get cracking on it now."

"Anyone else want to offer up any suggestions?" Hero scanned his team. Their mumblings amounted to a big fat zero. "Okay, carry on then, guys. Let's keep digging and checking on the folks involved. I'll get onto the path lab."

Hero walked in the direction of his office but turned when he sensed someone behind him. "Everything all right, Foxy?"

"Yes, sir. I wanted a private chat with you."

"You better come in my office then. Coffee?"

"Yes please. White, one sugar."

Hero dropped the coins in the vending machine then carried the cups into the office, kicking the door shut behind him. "Is this about the instructor?"

"It is, sir. Frank asked around the rest of his team to see if they'd heard anything detrimental about Wade, and he was shocked to learn that the instructor has been in bother before."

"You mean the same sort of thing my sister is going through?"

"Yes, sir. Frank heard rumours that on two separate occasions Wade wasn't able to keep his hands off the female recruits."

"Jesus. What am I supposed to do about this, Foxy? What happened to the two women involved in the complaints?"

"For a start, sir, neither woman put in a complaint about him."

"What? Why?"

Foxy pulled a look that said, 'You should know better than to ask a dumb question like that.' She shrugged. "Both women ended up leaving the training centre and chucking in their careers."

"Wow, really? Were they any good? What I'm trying to say is we know how vigorous the training can be. Was their leaving wholly due to an incident involving Wade, or did they simply find the training too much to handle?"

"I guess we'll never know, sir, unless..." Foxy smiled slyly.

"Unless someone pays them a visit. Is that what you're getting at?"

"Yes, sir. I'd be willing to carry out the task. That is, if you sanctioned it."

"Hmm... let me think that over for a while and get back to you, Foxy. What with Julie's unfortunate domestic circumstances throwing a spanner in the works, we're going to be short staffed around here. Therefore, all our resources should be concentrated on the murder enquiries we're dealing with, not trying to get one over on an instructor who touched up my sister."

"I understand, sir. The offer still stands if you want to revisit the situation in the near future."

"I appreciate that, Sally. Did Frank say anything else? Has this Wade been in bother with any of the male recruits, for instance? Not for touching them up. I meant for any form of bullying perhaps?"

"Frank hadn't heard, but talking to one of his team, he found out that a few of the male recruits had jacked in their training, too, giving feeble excuses when asked the reasoning behind their decisions."

Hero's eyes widened. "Are you thinking that they were bullied?"

"That, we don't know. You know how it goes, boss. If people aren't willing to speak openly about something like this, then any speculation won't see the light of day. Who's going to be the one to start a rumour? Another recruit? Not likely, due to the threat of repercussions from Wade."

"You have a valid point there. Something has got to be done to stop this Wade bloke. Okay, thanks, Foxy. I'll think things over and try to come up with a plan to reel the bastard in."

Foxy rose from her seat to leave and picked up her cup of coffee. Before she left the room, she turned and said, "A word of warning, sir. He comes with a mean reputation and a hell of a violent temper."

"Does he now? That's all the more reason to bring him down then, isn't it? How in God's name was he given a training role with a rep like that?"

Foxy shrugged. "Precisely. If you need either my help or Frank's, let me know. People like that shouldn't be in the force as a trainer, or in a training role anywhere else, come to think of it."

Hero was still contemplating paying Wade a visit when Jason knocked on the door. "Come in, Jason."

"Sir, I've done a bit of a background check on the landlord and couldn't find anything out of the ordinary in his past. Upon reflection, if there had been anything, his licence would've been revoked, wouldn't it?"

"There is that. Are you and Lance up for doing some more surveillance?"

"Sure. On Cathy Daws?"

"Yes, let's see what she gets up to during the day when she's not at work. That might tell us something or lead us somewhere we haven't thought of searching before."

"Do you want us to set off now?"

"You might as well. Get in touch with me as soon as she's on the move, all right?"

"Yes, boss."

Once his office was empty again, Hero reached for the phone and dialled the pathology lab. "Gerrard, hi. It's Hero. What do you have for me?"

"On what exactly? Because I know damn well you wouldn't be insane enough to give me a call about last night's incident. It would be *far* too soon to expect crucial information like that."

Hero cleared his throat and held back a snigger. He'd always been on reasonably good terms with Gerrard Brown over the years, but sometimes, the man's unintentional sharp tongue amused him. "No, not necessarily about last night's incident. I just wondered if you had anything extra for me, full stop. What about from Lomax, the body found in the tunnel?"

"I'm glad to hear it. Right, let me see, there was something of interest that came to light I seem to recall, just a sec."

Hero tapped his pen on the desk while he heard the pathologist cussing on the end of the line as he rummaged through the files on his desk. The man even managed to drop the phone once or twice, almost deafening Hero.

"Here we are. Right, sorry to keep you waiting, Hero. Further results from the man found in the tunnel, Lomax, have concluded that another set of prints were found on the body."

"Really? Where?"

"On the man's belt, I believe."

"I don't suppose you've had a chance to run the prints through the system yet, have you?" Hero asked, more in hope than expectation.

"We did, as it happens, they resulted in a negative. I'll send a copy of the file over to you if you like. It'll be handy for you to have at the station in case you pick up a suspect. How's the case progressing? Any major suspects at present?"

Hero let out a long breath. "Well, it's kind of frustrating. We've got our eye on a suspect. The trouble is she has cast-iron alibis for when the bloody murders were committed."

"Can she be connected to all the crimes?"

"Yes, that's the frustrating part. She knew all the victims. One of them, Stuart Daws, was even her husband. If we can pin last night's attack on her, we could be home free. The thing is we've already checked with her employer, and he says that she was at work when Foster was attacked."

"Ouch, that's not so good. Could she be getting someone else to kill the people for her, in that case?" Gerrard asked after a few seconds of silence.

"Initially, I would have said yes, especially with regard to the husband's death. God knows we see enough of that type of thing, don't we? I had my suspicion that she even recruited Foster to kill the husband. His car, or a car similar to his, followed Daws right before he was murdered. Now I'm not so sure."

"Why?"

"Well, for one thing, she can't keep befriending people to do her killing for her and then bump them off once they've outlived their usefulness, can she?"

"It's not unheard of. I mean, that type of crime has gone on in the past. It might be worth delving deeper into, given that she always seems to have credible alibis."

"You could be on to something. Maybe I'll call her in for another round of questioning. Thanks Gerrard. I don't have to tell you how important it is to rush the results through for the Foster case, do I?"

"No, you don't. Talk soon."

Hero hung up and contemplated what to do next. Jason and Lance were already watching Cathy, so maybe it would be wiser to hold off bringing her in for questioning for the next day or two?

Jason and Lance returned to the station once Cathy had clocked in for her shift at the pub during the afternoon. Jason shrugged and shook his head when Hero asked what they'd seen.

"Nothing. She didn't even leave the house to pop out for a pint of milk. No visitors, nothing."

Hero pulled a face and scratched his head. "Bummer. I'm really not sure what we're bloody missing here. There's got to be something. All right, gang, let's call it a day and start afresh tomorrow. We'll go over every tiny detail until something jumps out and bites us in the butt. Goodnight, all."

He watched the team gather their coats and leave for the night. Then Hero went back into his office, and before he finished for the day, he rang his partner to see how things were with her mum.

After six rings, she finally answered. "Julie? It's Hero. How's your mum?"

Julie let out a shuddering breath. "She's gone."

Hero swept a hand over his face and fell back in his chair. "Christ, I'm so sorry. Is there someone there with you?"

"No, I don't want anyone here. I just want to be left alone." With that, she hung up.

As much as he didn't take kindly to her hanging up on him, he totally understood the need for her to distance herself from the outside world. Julie had been very close to her mum, and Hero feared how she would cope with the loss. He would ensure that he cut her some slack and allowed her the space, and time, to grieve.

Hero pulled on his jacket and made his way through the building. In the car park, he rang Fay and told her that he had to make a slight detour on his way home. Within twenty minutes, he pulled up outside the training centre. He sat there, observing the comings and goings of both the recruits and uniformed officers for the next ten minutes, until he spotted the person he was after. When Wade left the building and got into his vehicle, Hero's heart pounded. He could feel his pulse beating a drum-like rhythm in his neck as he followed Wade's car out of the car park, mindful to keep enough distance between the two vehicles so as not to alert the man that he was tailing him.

They travelled across the city and towards the Eccles area. Seeing Wade slow down and pull into the driveway of a 1930s semi, Hero drove past and parked his car in a nearby parking space. He switched off the engine and twisted in his seat to look behind him. Hero was surprised to see a blonde woman in her early forties open the front door and greet Wade with a hug. The instructor shared a long kiss with the woman, which, for some unknown reason, sickened Hero. *So he's married, and still, he likes to touch up the girls, does he? Well, I'll have to see what I can do about that, won't I?*

"Mess with my family, mate, and you better be prepared to suffer the consequences."

Hero drove home and arrived just as Fay was putting Louie to bed.

"You're late, love." Fay was holding Louie's hand. The sleepy boy lifted his chin to accept Hero's kiss.

"Sorry, Fay, I had a detour to make. I'll tell you all about it once this cheeky chappy is tucked up in bed. How have the girls been today?"

"We've looked after them well together today, Mummy, didn't we?" Louie piped up.

"You've been an excellent help, sweetie. I'm most grateful. Now let's go and tuck you in. Hero, put the kettle on. I'm dying for a cuppa."

Hero flicked the switch on the kettle, greeted Sammy, then let the dog out into the back garden. The dog ran past him and returned carrying a tennis ball.

"Drop it then."

The dog dropped the ball but quickly pounced on it before Hero had the chance to pick it up. He ruffled the dog's head. "One of these days, you'll learn to retrieve and leave it like any normal dog. Go on, off with you and do your business."

Fay joined Hero as he was tucking into the evening meal he had heated up in the microwave. "Sorry if it's spoilt. I hope the pastry isn't too soggy?" She poured the coffee and sat down next to him.

"It's fine. You worry too much."

Fay took a sip from her mug of coffee before she asked, "Why are you so late?"

"First of all, I have some bad news to share."

"What?"

"Julie's mum died in the hospice today. She took a turn for the worse overnight. I'm really not sure how Julie is going to cope over the next few weeks. She was extremely close to her mum."

"Maybe the force can set up some kind of counselling for her. I am sorry. That's a bitter pill to swallow. I know how much losing Dad knocked me off my axis. Send her my best wishes the next time you talk to her, won't you? It's tough losing a parent."

"I will. *Then*, I heard that this Wade guy—you know, Cara's instructor—has been up to no good with a few of his other pupils, and I decided to follow him home."

"What are you talking about? Other sexual harassment charges?"

"No, it never went that far. The two girls involved left the force. But I also heard that he's been bullying the male recruits, too."

"That's appalling, Hero. What can you do about it?"

He smiled. "What I always do in cases like this. I intend getting to the bottom of it."

CHAPTER FOURTEEN

Hero stood at the whiteboard the following morning, awaiting his team's arrival. "Come on, guys. Let's get cracking."

Lance was the last of the team members to join them. He scurried to his seat and gave Hero an embarrassed smile.

"Okay, first of all, I have to impart some sad news. Before I left the office yesterday, I rang Julie. Sadly, her mother has passed away."

The team mumbled their sympathies.

Foxy raised her hand to speak. "That's a shame, sir. Do you want me to organise a whip round for a bunch of flowers? To let Julie know that we're thinking of her."

"Nice thought, Foxy. Everyone agreeable to that?"

The team all nodded.

"Right, now where were we yesterday? Lance and Jason carried out surveillance on our prime suspect, Cathy Daws, and returned with a disappointing result. I heard back from the pathologist that yet another set of prints were found on the victim from under the railway bridge. As yet, we have nothing to match them up to. I'm hazarding a guess they belong to Cathy. The thing is, we can't keep bringing her in for just questioning. We need something solid to go on. Any suggestions?"

"Do we have any DNA evidence which places her at Foster's flat, sir?" Jason asked.

"Not at the moment. It's too soon to get any results from the scene, and I didn't want to push my luck with the pathologist. He's got a lot on his plate right now. He'll give us the results as soon as he can. What else have we got?"

"Well, we do have the fact that the neighbours of Foster and Lomax picked Daws out in the photos they were shown," Foxy said, tapping her pen against her cheek as though she were thinking aloud.

"That's right. What are you thinking, Foxy? Ask them to come in for a line-up?"

"Yes, sir. Of course we'd have to bring the suspect in, too. That's why I hesitated bringing it up. You've already said that you can't keep yanking Daws in for questioning without a solid foundation for doing so."

"You're right, but I think this will be the excuse we're looking for. When she's here, we could fingerprint her, see if the prints match up to those found on the tunnel victim, Lomax."

"That's the line I was going down, too, sir," Foxy said.

Hero nodded. "Let's see what else we have first, and then we'll get this organised between us, Foxy. Has anyone got anything additional they want to offer? Come on, guys, there has to be more stones we've yet to peep under."

The room remained silent as the team members shook their heads.

Jason clicked his fingers together. "Did we ever find Lomax's vehicle, sir?"

"At the scene of his murder, you mean?"

Jason nodded. "Yes, sir."

"No, I don't think we've even looked for it yet. Good thinking, Jason. I'll leave that with you. Anything else?" When the group failed to offer any further suggestions, Hero said, "Okay, let's get to it, peeps. Foxy, a word in my office before we start, please?"

Foxy followed him through to the office and closed the door behind her. "Sir?"

"I just wanted to bring you up to date on the other matter we discussed yesterday. Take a seat."

They sat at his desk. Hero placed his elbows on the table and rested his chin on his fists. "I did something last night that some of our superiors might deem as foolish."

"Uh-oh, I'm not liking the sound of that, sir."

He reclined in his chair and grinned. "It wasn't that bad. Actually, I'm pretty pleased with myself for the restraint I showed."

"Are you going to let me in on what you did, sir?"

Hero chuckled. "Okay. Well, after I rang Julie last night, I left the station, and for some strange reason, my car chose a different route home."

Foxy smirked and shook her head. "Uh-oh, I think I know where this is leading. Pray tell me, sir, where did your vehicle take you?"

"To the training centre. Fancy that, eh? Anyway, I waited for a good ten minutes before I spotted the person I was looking for. I followed Wade home, and imagine my surprise when Mr. Wade gets out of his car and shares a loving embrace with his wife. At least I'm presuming she was his wife."

"Never! Ew… I feel deeply sorry for her living with a creep like that. Tell me you didn't do anything rash, like confronting him in front of her."

"Grant me with some sense. No, I just wanted to see what I was up against. I'm biding my time before I hit him, so to speak. I think we should definitely organise a visit with his other victims though, don't you? The sooner, the better. Maybe see how the day progresses with Daws first. Can you get the two women's details for me, for us, to pounce on once we're clear of this case?"

"I'll do it right away, sir. Do you want me to make the arrangements for the witnesses to come in sometime today, too?"

"Yes, do that. We'll probably have to send a car out to both Mrs. Taylor and Mr. Wilson. Let's get that arranged for this afternoon around three, all right?"

"Won't Cathy Daws be at work then, sir? She generally starts her shift at the pub around that time, doesn't she?"

"Precisely. I'm going to wait until she's at work and pick her up from there. Let's stir things up a little, eh?" Hero winked at Foxy.

She stood up to leave. "I like your line of thinking, sir. I'll start the ball rolling on this lot then and get the collection started for Julie, too."

Hero dug out his wallet and handed Foxy a ten-pound note. "Here you go. This will get you off to a good start."

"That's generous of you, sir. I'm not sure the others will be giving up that much of their pay packet."

"That's okay. Just tell them to put in what they can afford. I'll make up the difference. Buy something decent for Julie. Let's show her how much we care and value her contribution to the team, eh?"

Foxy pulled open the door. "Leave it with me. I'll get back to you within the hour, sir."

Hero nodded. He puffed out his cheeks and began sorting through the post littering his desk.

True to her word, Foxy knocked on his door within the hour.

"Come in and take a seat, Sally."

She placed her notebook on the desk and started reading from her notes. "First things first. The team did us proud, sir. We managed to scrape together fifty pounds for Julie. I've placed the order with Interflora. They promised me that they would deliver the bouquet early this afternoon."

"Excellent, I'll be sure to thank the team for their generosity. Anything else?" He nodded for her to continue.

"Mr. Wilson was adamant that he couldn't come in until his lunch had gone down. He actually said 'passed through,' which was a little too much information. I told him that someone would collect him at two thirty."

Hero laughed. "You have my permission to shoot me if I ever get to be his age and turn out to be as crotchety as he is."

"Yes, sir. I'll make a note of it. Mrs. Taylor was lovely about coming in to help out. She wanted to remind you of your promise, though, about cleaning up the area."

"They always want something in return. I was mulling over her circumstances last night and thought I might ring a contact of mine at the housing department. It would be nice to see the old dear settled in a safe area. It can't be fun living alone and on your nerves like that." Picking up his pen, he pulled a scrap piece of paper in front of him and jotted down a note for himself.

"I agree. It would be nice if you could get her moved. I'm sending another car to pick her up around the same time as Mr. Wilson. What do you want to do about Daws?"

"Well, if the two witnesses are coming in around two forty-five or thereabouts, I don't want to keep them waiting too long. Be ready for two fifteen. We'll go out and pick Daws up then. We'll be a nice surprise waiting for her when she turns up for her shift."

"I can see your evil streak on show, sir." Foxy laughed as she left the office.

Hero snatched up the phone and rang his contact at the local council to bend his ear about Mrs. Taylor's predicament.

"Hi, Todd. Long time, no hear. It's Hero Nelson."

"Hero, well, this is a surprise. I heard on the grapevine that you've just become a father. My sympathies to you."

Hero laughed. "Cheers, mate. I'm calling time on three kids. Couldn't cope with six kids like you and your missus. Jeez, the thought of never having a decent night's sleep again would make me want to kill myself."

"It ain't that bad. I keep a mallet beside their beds in case they wake up. Before you come over here and slap the cuffs on me, I'm only winding you up."

"Yeah, I thought you might be. I know how much those kids mean to you. Right, the reason I'm ringing is to see if you can help me out at all."

"I'll try my best, mate. What do you need?"

"Well… how about a nice home for a sweet widow in a safe area?"

"Are you kidding me? In Manchester?"

Hero replied, cringing, "That's what I was hoping, yes."

"A place such as that no longer exists, Hero. Even you should know that."

"I just thought I'd try and help out a witness. Can you do a little digging for me? Maybe, there's some kind of residential flat with some form of security."

"Not on our patch and nothing that is council owned. She'd need to stump up cash for a dwelling like that."

"See what you can do, please?"

"I will. It might take me a few days, but I'll do my best."

"Cheers, Todd. You're a star."

Hero hung up and glanced at the neighbouring buildings outside his window, lost in thought. His frustration mounted as he summarised the conversation he'd just had. What a terrible thing to say—there didn't appear to be a safe area at all within his region. Despite banging up criminals day in and day out, there was still far too much crime in the Manchester area for them to police adequately.

Shaking his head, he set about clearing his paperwork. There was no point dwelling on things out of his control. Hero had learnt that the hard way over the years. *Why couldn't I have chosen a quiet rural location in which to bring up my family? Maybe I should have a serious chat with Fay soon to see what her position is about them bringing the kids up in one of the roughest parts of the UK.*

Late morning, Hero sent Jason to collect sandwiches for the team, which they shared in the incident room while running over the final plans for that afternoon.

"Lance, you questioned Mr. Wilson. Therefore, I think it would be best if you picked him up after lunch."

"Yes, boss," Lance said then gulped the last of his coffee.

"Jason, I want you to bring Mrs. Taylor in, all right?"

"Yes, boss."

"As we're a man—I mean, a woman—down, I'll get control to divert any calls to another department until we all return. Foxy and I will be out picking Daws up. Right, we set off in ten minutes, guys. Let's make this count. I hope the witnesses come up trumps for us today."

CHAPTER FIFTEEN

During the course of the drive to the Dog and Duck pub, Hero's stomach flipped numerous somersaults as he anticipated Daws's reaction when they asked her to accompany them to the station. There was only one way to find out.

Hero and Foxy walked into the pub and approached the bar.

"Can I help you?" the man serving asked.

"Steve Gillan?" Hero flashed his ID at the man.

"It is. What can I do to help, Inspector?" He continued to wipe the glasses and place them in neat rows on the shelves behind him.

"I need to ask you a favour."

"Go on."

Hero looked around the near-empty public bar and lowered his voice as he leaned towards the landlord. "We're here to take Cathy Daws in for questioning. I know it's going to disrupt her shift, but we need to do so immediately, in light of new evidence that has come into our possession."

He angrily threw his cloth on the bar. "Jesus, I need to go out this afternoon, and I was relying on Cathy running the place in my absence. Couldn't you guys have done this earlier? Like this morning, when she was at home?"

"Sorry, our witnesses couldn't make it then. Can you arrange for another staff member to stand in for her?"

"I suppose so. I'll call Paula now. You guys want a drink while you wait? Cathy isn't due for another ten minutes or so."

"No thanks. We'll sit over here, out of the way."

"Whatever," the landlord grumbled as he left the bar and slipped into the back room.

Cathy Daws walked through the pub's entrance five minutes later and headed for the bar.

Hero called out to her before she reached it, "Cathy, we'd like a quick chat, if you don't mind?"

Cathy hesitated as if deciding whether or not to take flight. In the end, she retraced her steps and stood in front of them. "What do you want now? Do we have to do this here?"

"We've cleared it with your boss. We'd like you to come down the station for further questioning."

"What? Jesus, you guys don't let up, do you?"

"Not when it's a murder enquiry, Cathy, no."

"But I keep telling you I know nothing. Why isn't that sinking into your thick heads?"

"Less of the insults." Hero rose from his chair and marched over to the bar. "Mr. Gillan?" he called out, straining to see if he could see the landlord through the doorway.

The landlord looked flustered and out of breath when he returned. "I can't get hold of any of my other staff. Are you sure you can't put this off for another day?"

"Sorry, no. We're going now. Hopefully, we won't cause you too much inconvenience. We'll try not to keep Mrs. Daws for too long."

"Shit, this is totally annoying for me. Cathy, I'm sorry, but if this is going to be a regular occurrence, I'm going to have to reconsider you working here."

"Steve, you can't do *that*. I haven't done anything wrong. I need this job." She turned to snarl at Hero. "Why don't you just fuck off and leave me alone? In fact, if you don't back off, I'm going to come after you with a harassment charge."

Hero locked eyes with her. "Calm down, Mrs. Daws. We're only taking you in for questioning. If you want me to resurrect the assault of a police officer charge, I'd be happy to do so. Now, are you coming with us, peacefully?"

"Just go, Cathy. We'll discuss your work situation later," the landlord urged, looking around him sheepishly, fearing Cathy's foul-mouthed tirade had drawn unwanted attention from the few regulars.

Cathy's shoulders crumpled in defeat, and she turned to walk out the same way she'd just come in. "All right. I'm not happy about this, though. Not one bit."

Hero thanked the landlord and followed Foxy and Cathy out of the pub. "I'll jump in the back, sir, just in case," Foxy said, opening the back door and ushering Daws inside.

"Are you going to behave yourself, Cathy? Or do I need to put the cuffs on?" Hero asked at the woman's reluctance to get in the car.

Cathy grunted, slipped into the backseat, and folded her arms.

Hero winked at Foxy. "I'm taking that as an affirmative."

They drove back to the station, and as Hero was about to enter the car park, he noticed Jason parking his car. Mrs. Taylor was sitting in the rear. Hero quickly changed direction to avoid having the witness spot Cathy travelling in his car. "Slight detour is needed, I think."

Cathy tutted and glared at him in the rear-view mirror. Hero did his best to suppress the chuckle dying to escape as he took the car for a spin around the block. When he returned, the car park was empty of people, so Hero and Foxy escorted Cathy into the station.

"Is there an interview room free, Sergeant?" Hero asked the duty desk sergeant.

"There is, sir. Room Two. The duty solicitor is waiting for you."

The desk sergeant buzzed the security doors open and invited the three of them into the hallway.

Winking, Hero leaned in to whisper, "Are the others here yet?"

"Yes, sir. Ready and waiting."

Hero led the way to the interview room with Daws and Foxy right behind him. He shook hands with Cathy's solicitor. "Thanks for coming in at such short notice, Mr. Boulten."

"Let's hope this isn't a waste of everyone's time, Inspector," Boulten said brusquely.

He smiled at the solicitor and turned to the suspect. "Take a seat, Cathy. Foxy, will you do the honours and say the necessary for the tape?"

Foxy pressed the record button and announced the date, time, and the people present in the room. Then Hero began questioning Daws.

"Cathy, since our last meeting, have you either heard or seen anything of Stan Foster?"

A puzzled look pulled at her face. "No," she said adamantly.

"Not even to say a quick hello?"

Sighing heavily and folding her arms again, Cathy once more offered a firm response. "No."

"Well, we believe differently and have the evidence to back up our assumption. I'm going to ask you if you wouldn't mind giving us a sample of your DNA. Would you?"

She glanced at her brief, who nodded at Hero.

"What for? Do I have to? I know my rights."

"It would make things easier if you offered it, although I'd have no hesitation in seeking a court order to obtain one. Of course, that would mean you having to spend the next day or so in a police cell until that order came through. The choice is yours," Hero said.

Through gritted teeth, she replied, "Go on then, if I must."

Hero turned to Foxy. "Can you organise that for me please, Sergeant?"

Foxy stood up, announced she was leaving the room, and left the room to notify the doctor they'd arranged to be on standby. She returned before Hero had a chance to ask Cathy anything else.

Foxy announced her return to the tape then told Hero, "The doctor will be five minutes, sir."

"Good. Cathy, is there anything you wish to share with us?" Hero pressed the suspect.

"Like what? I keep saying I don't know this man."

"Well, we have reason to believe differently. All right, answer me this then, where were you the night before last at around eight in the evening?"

She shrugged. "That's easy—at work. And don't bother giving me any bullshit about checking my rota. I know full well that you've already asked my boss, right?"

"Yes, we have. Were you at the pub all evening? What about nipping out during your break? You do get a break, don't you?"

"Sometimes. It depends if Steve's got a function on or not. That night, he had a function—an out-of-town skittles team—so I didn't get a break."

Hero glanced at Foxy, and the uncertainty written on her face mirrored his own.

Someone knocked at the door, and Foxy leapt out of her seat to answer it. The doctor walked in, and Foxy introduced him to the tape.

"Can you take off your jacket, Cathy? So the doc can take some blood?" Hero asked.

She shook her head and her eyes grew wide. "You never said anything about wanting my blood. I'm scared of needles."

The doctor smiled to reassure her. "I promise I won't hurt you."

She stretched away from the doctor as he dipped into his bag to extract a fine-needled syringe. "No, I can't. I won't," the suspect insisted.

"Okay, doc, can we get the DNA another way? Perhaps a buccal swab?"

"If I have to. There's no need to be so petrified. It's like a cotton bud being put in your mouth, that's all," the doctor tried to assure Daws.

Cathy's eyes darted around at the other occupants of the room as she reluctantly nodded.

The doctor took out the swab. "Open wide."

When the doctor had finished he left the room. Hero shuffled forward in his chair. "While you're here, we'd like you to be involved in a line-up." He glanced at the solicitor, whose eyes remained on his notepad.

"What? What for?"

"All right, look at it this way. If you say you're totally innocent of the crime, then the two witnesses we've brought in won't pick you out, will they? Either you agree to the line-up, or again, we'll get a court order for you to go through with one. What do you say?"

"I say you're pissing me off. You're never going to believe me, no matter how much I protest my innocence, are you?"

"That about sums it up, Cathy. Are you ready?" Hero walked over to the door and looked back at the suspect, who was staring at the wall in front of her, stubbornly ignoring him. "I'll give you to the count of five. One... two... three... four..."

Cathy looked daggers at her brief, who hadn't halted the proceedings, and slammed her hands on the table, using them to lever herself to her feet. She stomped towards Hero, her face crimson with anger. "I'm only agreeing to this so I can look forward to watching the egg drip off your face."

Hero opened the door, inviting Cathy to leave the room ahead of him. "We'll see," he mumbled as she passed.

James Boulten remained in the room.

She snapped her head around to face Hero. "Yeah, we will."

Foxy and Hero walked alongside Cathy, steering her through the warren of corridors towards the room they used for line-ups. Hero opened the door and ushered Cathy to stand in line with five similar-looking members of the public they had managed to round up at short notice. He positioned the suspect in front of the number-four sign posted on the wall. "Just look natural and try not to scare the witnesses with that death stare of yours."

"You're hilarious." Cathy sneered.

Hero leaned in. "Do you think I missed my vocation, Cathy?"

The other people in the room sniggered, but Cathy just glared at him contemptuously.

After leaving the room, Hero stepped into the room next door to meet Mrs. Taylor. He shook hands with the tottering old lady. "How are you today, Mrs. Taylor?"

"Pig sick of being cooped up in my flat when the streets aren't safe to walk around it. Apart from that, I suppose I'm well."

Hero winked at her. "I had a word with a friend of mine at the council about your situation. I don't want to raise your hopes, but he's going to see what he can do to help out. I thought that would bring a smile to your face."

"Oh, it has, lovey. It's definitely done that. What do I have to do then? With regard to this, I'm talking about."

Hero motioned for Foxy to turn off the light. Once the room was pitch-black, Hero flicked a switch that allowed them all to observe the occupants of the room next door through the one-way mirror.

"Oh, what kind of magic is this?"

"It is pretty nifty, isn't it? Here we go then, Mrs. Taylor. As you can see, each of the women have a big number above their heads. I'd like you to simply tell me which number corresponds to the person you saw visiting Foster's flat. Do you think you can do that for me?"

Mrs. Taylor's eyes strained as her nose touched the glass, which didn't exactly fill Hero with confidence.

"Hmm... let me see. Can they maybe turn to the side?"

"Let me ask them. Please be quiet while I use the microphone." He pressed the button and bent down to use the mic. "Could you all please turn to your right?" He let go of the switch and watched the six women turn to face the wall. "What do you think? Do you recognise anyone now?"

"Now don't go shouting at me if I get this wrong. I think number four is the one you're after, but my eyesight isn't like it used to be."

"Would you like them all to turn the other way? Would that help?"

"I don't think so, dear." She nodded firmly. "I'm sticking with my answer, number four. She looks kind of a dubious character, so it was a no-brainer for me."

Hero turned and flicked the switch again, which sent the room next door into darkness and switched on the light to the room they were standing in. "Thank you, Mrs. Taylor. You've been most helpful. I'll get Jason to drop you back home now." He held out his hand and gently shook the lady's.

"Any chance your young man could play chauffeur with me and take me to the supermarket? What with me not being able to get out of my flat my cupboards, my fridge actually is looking pretty empty, and my daughter can't fit me in until the weekend."

"I don't see why not. One good turn and all that. Thanks for sparing the time to drop in and see us today." Turning to his partner, Hero said, "Sally, can you deliver Mrs. Taylor back to her allocated chauffeur and pick up the next witness?"

While Foxy was gone, Hero flicked the mirror back on and studied the suspect. Apart from anger, he couldn't really tell what was running through Cathy Daws's mind. She was looking down at her feet most of the time, ignoring the other women in the room. Or were they ignoring her? Hero couldn't really tell which way round it was, but Cathy was certainly set apart from the other occupants. Hero heard footsteps in the hallway and flicked the switch again.

Mr. Wilson entered the room and immediately dropped into the chair. "My legs have trouble holding me up at times. Mind if I take a second to catch my breath?"

"Not at all. Can we get you a tea or coffee?"

"Don't fuss on my count, sonny." He pulled himself upright in the chair and glanced around the room. "Well this is a funny little room. What goes on here then?"

Hero switched off the overheard light and illuminated the room next door. "To your places people, please?" he asked the women in the adjacent room. The women shuffled back beneath the numbers they'd been given and stood erect. He muted the microphone and turned to his second witness. "Right, Mr. Wilson, I'd like you to pick out the woman you thought you saw paying Lomax a visit."

Mr. Wilson rose to his feet and stumbled forward. After several silent minutes, he pointed a shaking finger at the woman standing beneath the number four. Cathy Daws.

"Are you definite about that, Mr. Wilson?"

"As sure as I eat Alpen every morning to help me... well, you know what I'm referring to. You're not daft. Although..." He frowned.

Here we go again. "Is there a problem, Mr. Wilson?"

"I thought I'd be able to pick her out, but now, I'm not so sure. What if I got it wrong? I couldn't live with myself for putting the wrong person in prison. Do you understand me?"

"Of course, I understand. Take all the time you need. There's no rush. I'll get the ladies to turn sideways for you, all right?"

Hero·put the request in and watched the ladies again turn to their right. He tried to bat away the sinking feeling in the pit of his stomach when Mr. Wilson peered at each woman and either shook his head or ran a worried hand through his snowy white hair.

"Anything?"

"If you're pushing me to make a guess, I'd lean towards saying number four, sticking to my original assumption. But again, I want to state for the record that I'm not one hundred percent sure she's the one."

"That'll be noted down, Mr. Wilson. No problem there." Hero extended his hand. "Thanks very much for taking the time and trouble to visit us today. Foxy will escort you out and put you in Lance's safe hands. I'll let you know the outcome of this case when it's concluded."

"Yeah, that'd be great. I'd like to know what happens. If it turns out not to be her in there, then I hope you catch the right person soon."

Foxy supported Mr. Wilson by the elbow as they left the room. Again, as he had before, Hero illuminated the room next door and scrutinised Cathy Daws's reaction.

When Foxy returned, she accompanied Hero back to the interview room.

"What happens next?" she asked.

"We say thank you to the people in the line-up and set them free."

Foxy stopped mid-step. "What? Even Cathy?"

"No. Sorry, I didn't make myself very clear, did I? Everyone else is free to go, but we need to put Cathy back in the interview room until I make a phone call."

"Do you want me to go and get Cathy now?"

"If you would. The desk sergeant can organise thanking the other line-up people and sending them on their way, while you make Cathy comfortable. Take a couple of coffees with you, for Boulten and Cathy, and tell them we need to question Cathy further. I'll be with you in a few minutes."

Hero took the stairs back up to the incident room two at a time and rushed into his office. He searched for the small address book he kept tucked at the back of his in-tray and looked up the number for his contact at the Crown Prosecution Service.

"Hi, Emily. It's DI Nelson."

"Hello there. How did it go?" Emily Grant asked, sounding a little distracted.

"Okayish. We called upon the services of two witnesses, old-timer witnesses, I hasten to add."

"Meaning?" Emily asked, seeming to have given Hero her undivided attention.

"Well, they've both said their eyesight isn't up to much nowadays. Not sure if that would stand up well in court."

"Yep, you have a point there. But they did pick the same person out. Is that right?"

"Yes. While the suspect was here—she still is here, actually—I asked the doc to take a DNA sample. The thing is the pathologist picked up further DNA evidence from one of the crime scenes. I'm banking on it matching Cathy Daws, but that will take a few days before it's verified," Hero said.

"We haven't got much to go on then, right?"

"Well, yes, there is that. However, another victim was murdered last night, someone else the suspect had a connection with. Just to recap, that's three murder victims, either known by or in a relationship with Cathy Daws. My greatest fear is that if we set her free, we could be having the same conversation tomorrow about yet another victim."

"I understand. What about alibis? Do they stand up?"

Hero exhaled a large breath. "Yep, that's the problem. Her boss confirmed she was at work during two of the murders."

"I can see exactly what the quandary is. It doesn't mean that she wasn't involved in the crimes, though, does it? She could've had help from another individual, such as her boss. Let me have a chat with someone, and I'll call you straight back."

"Thanks," Hero said before hanging up. While he waited for Emily to ring back, he took out his mobile and called his sister. "Hey, Cara. How are you doing?"

"How do you think I'm doing? I'm bored out of my mind. I keep sitting down one minute, pacing around the room the next. God, this is driving me crazy, Hero, just bloody crazy."

"I'm sorry you're going through this hell, love. Truly, I am. How about coming round for dinner tonight? I think I'll be wrapping up a case today. That's the plan anyway. What do you say? Louie would love to see you." Hero played the doting nephew card, hoping it would change his sister's mind. It wasn't good for her to be by herself at such an awful time.

"All right, I'll fold. Can I pop round to your place early, say about five? I could help Fay prepare the dinner or look after the twins while she gets on with it. I'm just going out of my mind here."

"Of course. I'll call Fay at lunchtime to tell her. Hey, Sis, keep your chin up. I have something up my sleeve that I intend putting into action soon." He cringed, regretting his mouth running away from him before he had a chance to engage his brain properly.

"Sounds ominous. Care to share?"

"Later, okay." His office phone rang, saving him further awkwardness. "Gotta fly. I'm expecting an important call. See you later." He picked up his landline. "DI Nelson."

"It's Emily again. After additional consultation, we've decided that it would be best for you to arrest the suspect, due to what you intimated earlier that there's a possibility of her or someone she's connected to carrying out more crimes of this nature. If we're wrong, then so be it. Let's get her off the streets now rather than regret it later."

Hero stood up. "Great, that's brilliant. I'll action that right away." He hung up then rushed downstairs and marched into the interview room. "Cathy Daws, I'm placing you under arrest for murder. Sergeant, would you do the honours of reading the suspect her rights?"

"Yes, sir."

As Foxy read Daws her rights, Hero watched the woman's reaction. Her mouth dropped open and she continuously shook her head until Foxy finished.

"I... I'm innocent. Why won't you believe me?"

"What?" Boulten spluttered. "I hope you know what you're doing, Inspector."

"I do, and frankly, I've heard enough crap for one day. Bang her up, Sergeant." Hero returned to his office, an elated feeling travelling through him at the speed of a Grand Prix racing car.

CHAPTER SIXTEEN

Just before he left for the evening, Hero received news that Cathy Daws had been shipped off on remand to Styal prison. During the afternoon, due to the way the Daws case had progressed, Hero had called Foxy into his office to discuss the other matter they were dealing with: Cara's unfortunate predicament.

"Foxy, now that's out of the way, I thought we could spend half an hour going over what we intend doing about Wade. I have Cara coming over for dinner tonight. It would be nice if I could give her some good news for a change. She sounded really down when I rang her earlier."

"That's a shame. Do you want me to give the two women who threw away their careers a call?"

"Yes. Them, and let's see if we can track any male recruits who left under suspicious circumstances, too. That way, we can offer a balanced view in case the authorities think we're going down the sexist route. We can ask them to take into consideration the way he treats *all* the recruits. What do you think?"

"Well, I have made an initial list to be getting on with. It would be better if we could tempt more people to come forward and speak out against Wade."

"If you can make a start this evening and finish it off in the morning, maybe we can make arrangements to interview some of these people tomorrow afternoon, before I take my paternity leave."

"Sure, I'll get started now." By the time she called it a day at the office, Foxy had managed to contact the two women as well as a couple of male recruits and arranged to either ring or visit them the following day.

Hero arrived home soon after six to an overexcited Louie, who was busy thrashing his aunt Cara on the Xbox. "Daddy, look. I made it to the next level. I've never been this far before."

Hero kissed his wife then Cara and Louie before he sat on the sofa next to his son. "Boy, you've done a fabulous job. I'm betting it was clever Auntie Cara who got you this far, though."

Mortified, Louie stopped playing and stared at him open-mouthed, momentarily lost for words. He soon realised that Hero was teasing him. He elbowed his father before continuing with his game. "Aww... Daddy! Watch this."

Hero winked at his grinning sister over the boy's head and mouthed, "Are you okay?"

Cara blew him a kiss. "Fine. Did you manage to wind up your case?"

Partially distracted by Louie's progress in the game, Hero informed his sister, "Yep, onto pastures new tomorrow."

Fay went through to the kitchen, calling over her shoulder, "Dinner in ten minutes, guys."

Hero tickled Louie, forcing the boy to relinquish his hold on the control. The pair ended up on the floor in fits of giggles as Cara watched on, laughing like a demented hyena.

"Come on, time to wash up." Hero jumped to his feet, swept Louie into his arms, and carried the giggling youngster upstairs to the bathroom.

During the meal, Hero kept the conversation light and teased Louie constantly. After they'd eaten, Fay bathed Louie, and while she put him to bed with a story, Hero had a serious chat with his sister about his plan.

"You can't do that, Hero." Cara chewed her bottom lip as his words sunk in.

"Of course I can. We can. Foxy and I are going to make a start on the interviews tomorrow. If these girls know this type of crap is still going on, I'm sure they'll step up to the plate and do what they can to help you."

"You have more faith in the human race than I do. If these girls haven't spoken up before now, there's fat chance of them considering doing it now."

"Ever the pessimist, dearest sister. These girls haven't been privy to my charm."

Cara put her head in her hands and groaned. "God help them!"

"Cheeky cow. It works all the time on women." He thought back to the suspect he'd just had carted off to prison and silently corrected himself. *Er... sometimes!*

"I really appreciate this, Hero. However I wish you'd reconsider. The last thing I wanted was for you to get involved in this and jeopardise your own career in the process."

"Nonsense. I'm determined to get this guy, Sis. His tactics can't be allowed to continue, not just for your sake. Think of all the other recruits starting out, having to deal with this bullying thug."

"That's a little OTT, Hero, but I get your drift."

"Right, enough of this chat. You're here to have some fun. Girl, I'm going to thrash your arse." He picked up the control to the game console and started a fresh game.

Cara laughed. "You can try, buster."

Hero walked into the incident room, feeling elated and ultra-excited about what lay ahead that day. "Morning, Foxy. Continue making all the necessary arrangements for this afternoon, will you, please?"

"It's all in hand, sir. I just have one more person to track down, and then we're good to go."

Hero nodded. "I'm impressed. I've got a few people to ring myself this morning, you know, to update them on the Daws situation. We'll grab a quick sandwich at lunchtime and shoot off after that, okay?"

"Fine by me."

He ventured into his office, pushed the post pile to one side, and began calling the people on his to-do list to inform them about Cathy Daws's arrest. Gerrard was his first call. The conversation was hurried but nevertheless jubilant. The pathologist promised Hero that they would rush the DNA sample through in spite of her arrest.

Hero went on to call both the witnesses whose valuable input the day before had made Cathy's arrest possible. Mr. Wilson and Mrs. Taylor were relieved, and both reminded Hero that one good turn deserved another. He made a note to do what he could to put the witnesses' minds at ease. The rest of the morning rushed by and resulted in Hero dealing with his paperwork, clearing his desk in record time. Arresting and charging a suspect had surprising effects on other areas of a copper's working life.

After treating the team to sandwiches, Hero and Foxy left the station and drove to Marie Lang's house. At first, the young woman was reluctant to let them into her tiny flat. However, she finally conceded, and the interview got underway.

"Marie, first of all, let me say that we're extremely grateful to you for putting yourself through this torment again. I'm also appalled that your plight wasn't dealt with appropriately at the time."

"I can't make any promises that my statement will stop this bastard. I'm willing to try, though. This man has to be stopped. I'm far stronger now than I was back then. Had it been different at the time, I wouldn't have hesitated to drag the bastard's good name through the mud." Marie shuddered. "God, the thought of him touching me… still makes my skin crawl. I lie awake most nights, scared to shut my eyes because all I see is that leer of his, taunting me."

"I understand. Hopefully, with yours and the traumatic statement of the other girl who is involved in this, we'll get the bastard kicked off the force as a minimum punishment. For the record, I admire and appreciate your bravery. I know this is going to be a hell of an ordeal for you to recap."

"It is. Providing the other girl goes ahead with her statement, I'm willing to stick my neck out to get this bastard back for ruining my career."

Foxy wrote out the statement as Marie told them about the events that led up to her running scared from the training centre and Wade. Hero's stomach churned at the despicable image the poor woman related to them in such a resolute manner. An unwavering passion to see justice prevail quickly replaced her initial reluctance. The woman's courage grew tenfold during the statement, and it was clear to Hero that Marie had conquered many demons since her ordeal two years before.

After everything was down on paper, Hero stood and shook the woman's hand, refusing to let go until he was certain that she accepted he would be doing everything in his power to deal with the sex-pest Wade.

"Thank you. Please let me know what happens. Also will you pass on a message to your sister for me?"

Hero released Marie's hand and smiled. "Of course. What's that?"

"Tell her that no matter how tough things get, to stick with it. She's lucky, in that she has you fighting her corner, giving her the strength needed to ensure this bastard no longer gets away with it. I had no one to back me up at the time. In the end, that proved to be my downfall."

"I'm sorry. That must have been hard to deal with, Marie. If it's any consolation, I sense, I mean, you come across as a well-adjusted young lady now. I'm glad you're finally putting this ordeal behind you and that you're able to get on with your life."

"Thank you. I have a good job now, one that I love and wouldn't change for the world. With you going after Wade, it'll be the icing on the cake for me to see him strung up by his balls."

Hero didn't feel the need to stifle his grin. "I can totally understand that sentiment, although the thought of it does bring tears to my eyes. Good luck, Marie. I think the Met will rue the day they let you slip through their fingers."

Marie's cheeks flushed. "Thank you. Wishing your sister strength and a successful outcome."

In the car, Foxy turned to Hero as he drove to the next witness's home. "I'm not sure I could have handled him trying to touch me up every single day, or the constant bullying. I bet he used the line on them that they better get accustomed to being treated disrespectfully, because that's what women had to deal with once they were out on the beat."

He turned to look at her. "Then you don't know yourself very well, Sally. I have a feeling if you'd come across the likes of Wade, you would've wiped the floor with him, especially if he shoved you in a supply cupboard and attempted to touch you up." He chuckled. "I also fear he wouldn't have any balls left to be hung by, if the force didn't back you up."

"There is that." Foxy laughed and pointed at the turning they should take.

They spent the next half an hour trying to coax the relevant information out of Claire Bosworth, who cried her way through the interview as she was forced to recount her own horrendous ordeal. When it was time to leave, Hero, himself on the verge of tears, promised the devastated young woman that he would personally see to it that Wade suffered for his role in destroying her confidence. The young woman, to this day, was finding it hard to come to terms with her ordeal. *What person in a trusted position had the right to destroy people's spirits like that?*

CHAPTER SEVENTEEN

Armed with the two women's statements as well as three men's statements, Hero dropped Foxy back at the station and drove off, telling her that he would see her bright and early the next day. He then drove out to the training centre and made himself comfortable while he waited for Wade to leave work. Twenty minutes later, the man walked out of the building and got in his car. Hero followed him, taking the same route to his home that they'd taken the previous time Hero had tailed him. About a mile from his house, Wade indicated and pulled into the curb.

Shit! He must've realised that I'm following him. What do I do now? Gulping down the saliva that had filled his mouth, he halted his own vehicle behind the man's and got out of the car.

Wade thrust his own car door open to challenge Hero. "Why are you tailing me? Who the fuck are you?" He flew at Hero, his face full of rage.

Hero stood his ground and pulled himself upright so that he was at least three inches taller than Wade. "I wanted to have a private chat with you."

"A chat? About what? And I asked who are you?"

"DI Nelson of the Met. You look surprised to hear that."

"You still haven't told me why you're following me."

"I wanted to have a talk with you, predominantly about my sister." Hero watched as Wade churned the name *Nelson* around in his head.

Suddenly, his eyes widened once he'd made the connection.

"Want to discuss that, Mr. Wade?"

"No, I do not. The case is due to be heard by a disciplinary panel shortly, I believe. You'll have to wait for the outcome. There's little I can do about things now."

"Ah, you're so wrong with that assumption, Wade." Hero folded his arms. "Here's how things are going to alter."

"Alter? Why should things alter? Your kid sister attacked me. End of, mate. Girls like that have no place in the force, in my book." His eyes fluttered shut and reopened as he shrugged.

"Hmm… okay. So it's all right for pervs like you to remain employed by the Met, is it?"

Wade stormed towards Hero, looking ready to strike him with his clenched fist.

"Go on, I dare you. My advice would be to make it a good shot, because it's the only one you're likely to get, mate." Hero laughed when the man rocked back and forth on the spot, as if hesitating before he carried out his threat. "Go on, why the hesitation? Oh yes, I forgot… idiots like you only feel at home intimidating students who can't fight back without getting disciplined, don't you?"

Wade turned away from Hero and marched back to his car.

Hero ran after him. "You're not leaving here until we've thrashed this out, moron."

"Get a life, Inspector. I have no plans of backing down on the statement I've made about your crazy sister."

"Crazy? Why is she crazy? Because she fought back where others let you get away with your secret groping frenzies?"

"You're insane. I've never had anything like this happen to me before. Check my record if you don't believe me."

"Oh, don't worry. I have. You know what, you're damn right. You're Mr. Squeaky Clean in the force's eyes. Except you're not, are you?"

"Prove it," Wade challenged with a smirk.

"The thing is, Wade, I *can* prove it. I'm here today to try and get you to see sense and to ask if you'll withdraw your complaint about my sister."

"Blackmail? How the heck can you blackmail me with lies?"

"Lies? So Marie and Claire and the male students we've got statements from are liars, are they?" Hero paused to let the names sink in. "Ahh… I see you're aware of who I mean. Here's the interesting part. I've spent most of the afternoon with these women, taking down very damning statements about why they felt obligated to quit the force. Hot damn, those accounts are on the verge of being included in the next Jackie Collins novel."

"Piss off. You're lying. I never touched those girls. It's all a bunch of lies. Come on, man, you know if you turn these girls' unwanted advances down, they'll do all they can to get payback."

"And that's what happened in Cara's case, is it? Because I know damn sure that she wouldn't give an ugly fucker like you the time of day."

The man's face dropped. Was that because he knew Hero had his balls in a firm grip? "Piss off. I've got nothing more to say to you." He tried to shut the door, but Hero lodged himself in the opening.

"The thing is, Wade, I know where you live…"

"This is harassment. I'll be speaking to my superiors in the morning about this unsavoury incident, Inspector."

"Well, that'll save me a job. Thanks for that. Meanwhile, I'm going to return to my car and follow you back to your house."

"Why? Give me a break, man."

"Well, I thought I would have a confidential chat with that stunning wife of yours."

Wade slumped forward, placed his head in his hands, and rested against the steering wheel.

Is that the sweet smell of success wafting up my nose? "You know what really galls me in all of this, Wade?"

"What?" Wade mumbled, still in the same position.

"The fact that you go home at the end of the day to a beautiful wife, and it's still not enough for you, is it? Now, are you going to reconsider your complaint, or do I pay your wife a visit tonight then stop by the training centre in the morning to see your superiors? These girls are willing to withdraw their statements if you drop the case against Cara *and* resign from your post."

"Jesus Christ… I can't do that. I'd wave goodbye to twenty years' pension."

Hero shrugged. "Either that, or I put these statements forward with the recommendation that the force shuts down the training centre, until a further investigation into yours, and possibly the other instructors' conduct, has been concluded."

He turned to face Hero at last, his eyes moist with frustration. "All right. You've got a deal. I want those statements before I retract my complaint, though?"

Hero laughed and shook his head. "What kind of fucking idiot do you take me for?" He walked away and called out. "Ring me tomorrow to let me know you've done the right thing, Wade." He jumped in his vehicle, carried out a three-point turn, and sped away. Looking back, he noticed that Wade had stepped out of his car and was pacing the road while running his hand through his hair.

The following morning, as Hero came within reach of the incident room, he heard a commotion coming from inside. He pushed open the door and shouted, "Guys, keep the noise down. What's going on?"

Foxy stepped forward, looking concerned. "We've had notification from the prison, sir, that Cathy Daws attempted suicide last night."

"Jesus! Attempted?"

"Yes, sir. She was rushed into hospital."

"Is she all right?"

"They're monitoring her. She tried to slit her wrists during her evening meal, but the guard found her before she lost too much blood."

"Crap, this could mean one of two things. Either she's innocent and found the situation intolerable, or it's a sign of guilt."

"Yes, sir. It could have been a cry for help," Foxy offered.

"Where is she now? Let's go and see if we can get to the bottom of this, Foxy."

"Salford Royal. I'll grab my jacket."

While Foxy went to her desk, Hero approached Lance. "I'm expecting a call from a Mr. Wade this morning. Give him my mobile number if he calls, will you?"

"Sure. What do you want the rest of the team to do, sir, in your absence?"

"Chase up any loose ends to the case."

Lance frowned. "Such as what, sir?"

"Use your head, man, for a change. Jason was trying to find out about Lomax's car. Follow up on that, for one thing. If Cathy Daws is innocent, then we still have a murderer out there. Let's be prepared to take the shit from the media for screwing up, okay?"

Lance nodded and looked embarrassed by the dressing down.

Foxy joined Hero, and they rushed out to the car.

"What's your gut telling you on this one, Foxy?" Hero asked once they were on their way to the hospital.

"To be honest, I think Cathy is innocent. She tried to commit suicide because she knows that despite having a solid alibi, everything is pointing to her being the guilty party."

"What about the witnesses? They indicated she was the culprit during the line-up, don't forget."

"Reluctantly, sir," Foxy rightfully pointed out.

Hero spent the rest of the journey contemplating how to handle Cathy when he arrived at the hospital. He would need to treat her with kid gloves.

Hero flashed his warrant card at the prison officer sitting outside Cathy Daws's private room, explaining that he was the arresting officer. The man granted them access to the room.

Cathy Daws's face was pale as she glanced their way when Hero and Foxy walked in. One of her arms was cuffed to the bed, and a nurse who was fiddling around with the IV drip stopped what she was doing when the door opened. She moved to the bottom of the bed to check Daws's chart.

"Hello, Cathy," Hero said.

Cathy mumbled a response. Her gaze shifted nervously between the two detectives and the nurse.

"Why did you do it, Cathy?"

She glanced at Hero for a split second then at the nurse before turning to look out the window.

"Cathy? Come on, share with us? I'm sorry you felt compelled to do such an awful thing."

Cathy's head swivelled towards him again, and she began to shake it slowly. "I'm innocent, I said. I've told you that right from the beginning." She snuck a look at the nurse before her gaze settled on her clenched hand lying in her lap.

Hero thought about asking the nurse to leave so they could talk freely, but one look at Cathy's pallor made him reconsider. Maybe it would be best to have someone with medical expertise on hand, just in case Cathy's recovery faltered during the questions he wanted to put to her.

"Is that why you tried to… well, harm yourself? Because you're innocent?"

Cathy sighed heavily, and when she looked up at him, her eyes were moist with tears. She forced out one word: "Yes."

"All right, Cathy, then tell us who the murderer is?" Out of the corner of his eye, Hero saw the nurse replace the chart and move over to look out of the window. When his attention returned to Cathy, she was watching the nurse, too. "Cathy, we can't help you if you won't trust and confide in us. Who did it?"

Cathy continued to stare past the nurse, out the window, until her eyelids started to droop. She struggled to keep them open, then her hand flew up to her chest, and her breathing became erratic.

"Do something!" Hero demanded of the nurse.

She remained fixated to the outside world and refused to help her patient. She seemed to be trying her hardest to suppress a smile. He reached for the panic button above Cathy's head and ran around the bed to try to shake the nurse into action.

Hero cried out and stumbled back, clutching his side. Foxy darted for the nurse and knocked the knife out of her hand before the woman could stab her, too. She called out, "Help! Help me in here."

The prison guard rushed into the room.

"Stop her. The nurse, restrain her," Foxy said, scrambling to ease Hero into the only chair in the room. "Hang in there, sir. I'll get help."

The guard gripped the nurse in a bear hug.

The doctor who'd answered the panic button call ran into the room. Alarmed, he asked, "What the hell is going on in here?"

Hero, fighting for breath, pointed at Cathy. "Check her, doc. When we came in here, the nurse was tampering with the drip."

The doctor rushed around the bed and pulled out the line. "What did you give her? Wait a minute, who are you? I don't recognise you. What are you doing here?"

The nurse snarled, "Putting her out of her miserable existence. She wanted to die. I was helping her with that wish."

With the line withdrawn, Cathy began to recover a little.

Hero asked her, "Cathy, do you know this woman?"

Cathy nodded slowly. "She's my sister."

Hero's mouth dropped open. "You said you didn't have any family. Why didn't you mention her?"

"To me, she was dead. I didn't know she was around until today. I swear," Cathy pleaded, stifling a yawn.

"Yeah, like you were dead to me. I told you I'd get revenge one day. Well, baby, that day has come, over and over again these past few weeks. Men, they're such dicks, easily led, most of them. Show them a bit of pussy, and they're game for anything."

"What the heck are you talking about? Stuart never mentioned that he knew you."

"Well he wouldn't, would he? I bet you didn't know he liked to spend all your hard-earned cash on prossies, did you?"

"You? A prostitute?" Cathy shook her head in disbelief.

"Yeah, when it suited. Like I said, I got my revenge after all these years. No one does the dirty on me."

"Foxy, call for backup." Hero tried to straighten up, but blood continued to pour out of the hole in his side.

"My God! You're wounded. Let me help you." The doctor rushed to tend to Hero's side, and the nurse used the distraction to wriggle free for a second. She pounced on Cathy and started slapping her face and beating her chest with her fists until Foxy and the guard restrained the nurse again. Foxy slapped the handcuffs on the woman's wrists. She wouldn't be escaping again.

"Cathy, what's her name?"

Welling up again, Cathy said, "It's Candy, Candy Drake. She's my half-sister."

Hero clicked his fingers, and Foxy turned his way. "The last word Foster said was 'Ca...'." I'm sorry, Cathy. I presumed he meant that you had attacked him. He was obviously trying to tell me it was Candy, not Cathy."

"He was a waste of space who I doubt is going to be missed anytime soon." Candy laughed a sick, demented laugh that seemed to rebound off the sterile white walls.

"And what about Lomax? Why did you kill him?" Hero asked, wincing as the doc studied and prodded at his side.

"Yeah, him, too. I used him to do the jewellers, him and that dipshit of a husband of hers, and they both screwed up. Lomax effing took his mask off. He had to be killed."

Hero's eyes narrowed at the cold, calculated way the woman recapped the events. "And Stuart Daws? Did he help you kill Lomax?"

"Yeah, he had an incentive to help me kill him." She laughed again.

"And that was?"

"Because he got greedy. He wanted Lomax's share of the money when the idiot had messed up. All men get greedy in the end."

"Keep still," the doctor said, tugging at Hero's arm.

Hero groaned and slumped back in the chair. "So that was you in the alley? You killed Daws?"

"Yeah, what about it? She shouldn't have done what she did all those years ago. If she hadn't treated me so despicably back then, none of this would've gone down."

Hero studied the woman. She was Cathy to a T. The resemblance explained why the witnesses thought Cathy was the woman who'd visited Lomax's and Foster's homes. It was all finally slotting together at last.

"So let me get this right. You killed Lomax first, and Daws witnessed that murder, so you killed him. *Then* because Foster knew about you murdering Daws, you got rid of him, too."

"If my hands weren't cuffed, I'd applaud you. It's a shame you didn't figure it out sooner, eh, Cathy?"

"Why? You mentioned you wanted revenge. For what?" Hero asked.

"Ask her." Candy motioned with her head in her sister's direction.

Cathy shook her head, refusing to speak up.

"She thought it was a huge joke at the time. Well, who's had the last laugh now, Cathy, eh?" she spat at her sibling.

"I'm sorry. I had no control of what he was going to do to you," Cathy stated.

"Yeah, well you had plenty of time to stop it. Instead, you pissed yourself laughing, didn't you?"

"I'm sorry," Cathy repeated sheepishly. "I thought he was messing around. We were all drunk. I had no idea he was going to tie you up and rape you."

Candy shuddered and Hero shook his head in disbelief. "What? Am I hearing this right? Your boyfriend raped your sister, and you allowed him to do it?"

Cathy covered her face with her hands. "He also abused and raped me. How could I have stopped him? I tell you… I couldn't. Nothing I could've said or done would've made any difference."

Hero winced again and slapped the doctor's hand away. "I don't know which one of you I feel more sorry for. You're both sick."

The doctor rose to his feet and dragged Hero with him. "This can wait. Your bleeding can't. Come with me."

Hero placed his arm on Foxy's as he passed. "Deal with this, Sergeant. I won't be long."

"Yes, sir. I've got it all in hand. You just let the doctor patch you up."

EPILOGUE

At work a few days later, Hero, still feeling relatively sore from being stabbed, had insisted on returning to work to tie up the case.

The team cheered when he pushed through the incident room doors. Even his partner Julie was there to greet him. "Hello, sir, welcome back."

"You, too, Julie. I'm glad to see you back where you belong. Everything all right?"

"I'm getting there."

They heard the phone ringing in his office. Gingerly, he made his way in there to answer it. "Hello, DI Nelson. How can I help?"

"So you're back then?"

"Is that you, Gerrard?"

"It is. Not affected your observation powers then? I heard about the stabbing. Are you all right?"

Hero chuckled. "Yep, it turned out to only be a nick. It's still pretty sore, though. What can I do for you?"

"It's more what can I do for you, Inspector. I have the results from the DNA samples. They're *not* a match."

"Now there's a surprise," Hero said, exhaling a relieved breath.

"Meaning what? I don't understand?"

"We caught the real culprit. It turned out to be Cathy's half-sister, Candy."

"Ah, that explains it," Gerrard told him with a tut.

"What? What am I missing here?"

"The mitochondrial DNA is the same. I take it they have the same mother?"

"Ahh… I see. Well, we're going to be questioning them both fully over the next few days. They're in custody. That's the main thing."

"So, it was a double act. Is that what you're saying? Because that's not what the DNA is telling us."

"No. But something happened in the women's past that led Candy to exact her revenge on her sister. Cathy will be charged with an accessory charge for that distant crime, and we're in the process of trying to trace her ex-boyfriend, so that we can throw the book at him, too."

"I wish I hadn't asked now. I'll leave you to get on with it then. Toodle pip for now."

Hero was still smiling when he hung up. He hadn't even started on his paperwork when his mobile rang. He answered it promptly when he saw the name on the caller ID. "Hey, Sis. How's it going?"

"Wonderful. It's so much nicer here now that Wade has gone."

"That's great, sweetheart. And the rest of the group are all right towards you? You're not getting flack for being a snitch?"

"No. If anything, they're acting like I'm their best buddy. It turns out, he's touched up a lot of the women in the class, but none of them had the courage to speak up about it."

"Whoa, really? Just goes to show, doesn't it? Well, tell them not to worry. Wade will get what's coming to him. I know he's resigned, but I've decided to make sure the proper authorities know exactly what he was up to. Will you be okay to give evidence against him?"

"Too right. I'm sure the others will be prepared to give evidence against him, too, if I ask them."

"That's excellent news and a great end result all round."

Hero hung up and reclined in his chair, wincing as the stitches in his side pulled tight. "An excellent end result indeed." Touching his side he added, "Almost."

NOTE TO THE READER

Dear Reader,

Thank you for joining in with the investigation. Did you guess who the killer was?
Do you want to get involved in yet another unputdownable Hero case?
In the next book Hero is hunting a violent killer with a heinous personal agenda.
He targets innocent people which include some of Hero's colleagues.
Join him in his next adventure here:

https://melcomley.blogspot.com/p/in-plain-sight.html

Thank you for your support as always.
M A Comley

P.S. Reviews to an author are like nectar from the Gods.

KEEP IN TOUCH WITH THE AUTHOR:

Twitter

https://twitter.com/Melcom1

Blog

http://melcomley.blogspot.com

Facebook

http://smarturl.it/sps7jh

Newsletter

http://smarturl.it/8jtcvv

BookBub

www.bookbub.com/authors/m-a-comley

Made in the USA
San Bernardino, CA
16 July 2020